This is Volume 2 Steve

Garden of Secrets

A Jack and Mira Adventure

Stephen M. Meritt

Storyline by Mira L. Sume

Printed in Jacksonville, FL, USA.

ISBN 10: 1610630306
ISBN 13: 987-1-61063-030-6

Library of Congress Control Number: 2015900998

Published by OnLineBinding.com

OnLineBinding.com
The Complete Solution

1817 Florida Ave
Jacksonville, FL 32206
Phone: 904.674.0621
Fax: 904.356.3373
Email: info@onlinebinding.com

STEPHEN M. MERITT

(Jack and Mira Adventure Series)

Dedication

For Mira, Grayson and Henry

Prologue

Several months had passed since Jack and Mira went on their adventure to Paradise, Arizona. Oh, what a trip it was! Jack had fallen into a mine shaft and while trying to get him out Mira had to deal with a wolf. She was already very nervous about dogs having been bitten once. The wolf turned out to be a lonely lost young pup that ended up helping lift Jack out of the mine. They fell in love with the pup and called him Nugget. He adopted Jack and Mira as his pack so they brought him home in the tornado. He turned out to be mostly wolf and part dog, but ten times smarter and huge. He was taller than Jack and Mira and came almost to the shoulders of an adult when he was on all fours.

Jack thought he had developed the gift of creating the traveling tornado. Once when he was all alone at the park near his home, he wished for an adventure. He was sucked up into a tornado and taken back in time to witness a Civil War battle. He was lucky to get back in the tornado and get home without being hurt.

Jack told his best friend and next door neighbor Mira about his adventure. Mira and Jack began to experiment with traveling in the tornado. First they went to Florida to fish with her Grandfather. Then they went to Norway to see a reindeer farm and watch a royal parade.

While on their adventure to Paradise, Mira began to hear whispers that Jack couldn't hear. It turned out that the tornado was not caused by Jack, but by Mariah, the Wind Maiden. She was a spirit of the Earth who had become lonely and found Jack in the park one day. She gave him a ride in a tornado and had been following him around when she met Mira. She had tried in the past to communicate with humans and animals but few could hear her. She could understand them, but had a really difficult time getting them to understand her. She had no physical form so she couldn't speak aloud. She could only speak mind to mind.

Mira, however, had a very unique mind and was able to hear and understand Mariah. It also seemed that Mariah could acommunicate with Nugget and told Mira not to worry about the wolf, whom she called El Lobo. Mira didn't tell Jack about Mariah at the time. She didn't want to upset her friend. After all, Jack was very proud of his new ability to control a tornado. Mira thought it best to let Jack continue to think that he was in control. There would come a time when it would be appropriate to let him know about Mariah. She knew he would also be upset that he couldn't hear her.

Chapter 1

Spring had arrived and Nugget was resting in the backyard of Jack's house. It was a typical spring day in West Hills. It was cool in the morning and hot in the middle of the day. Nugget had just taken a quick dip in Jack's pool and was now enjoying the warm sun. In a few minutes he would move to the shade of the flowering pomegranate tree with its pretty red flowers.

Nugget knew that Jack and Mira would not be home for several hours. They were at school and soccer practice. So he would spend his day resting and watching over his pack leaders' homes. The adults were all away and would return later with his Alphas. That's how Nugget thought of Jack and Mira. They were the male and female leaders of his pack. He was their loyal follower. He would do anything they wished. He was a very smart wolf.

He still thought of himself as a wolf. Actually, he was a wolf dog. His Mother was a sand colored Labrador and his Father a Mexican Gray Wolf. It is very rare for a wolf to take a dog as a mate, but the wolf was young and alone and wanted to start a pack of his own. When Nugget's Mother died his Father brought the young pup into another pack. All was fine until Nugget grew bigger. He was bigger even than the other wolves. They ran him out of the pack and he was forced to live on his own. Getting food for a lone wolf is very difficult. He was on the verge of starving when he found Jack and Mira. He watched them and encouraged by a hint from Mariah, helped them with a rope game. He helped pull Jack from a mine shaft. They gave him food and he decided that they would be his new pack.

He was very glad that he chose Jack and Mira. They turned out to be very loving and he loved them. They took him for walks in his new territory and fed him very well. So well, in fact, that he had grown to his full potential as a very tall and strong wolf. He was much larger and stronger than the average wolf. No dog could match him. Jack noticed this one day when he took Nugget to the dog park. If Nugget stood beside an ordinary dog it was like a Chihuahua standing next to a St. Bernard.

The dog park was a comfortable area with a five foot fence surrounding a grassy area. There were obstacles for dogs to jump over, or climb. It was very similar to a human park. Jack brought Nugget there one day and told him to be sure to behave. He didn't know how the other dogs would react. Nugget understood what Jack meant and would not cause any trouble. Jack always walked Nugget on a leash even though it wasn't necessary. Nugget was always well behaved. It was the law that all dogs must be leashed, but in the dog park they could run free.

Jack brought along a tennis ball which Nugget loved to catch. If Jack threw it far, Nugget would fetch it and return it to Jack. Sometimes, Jack would bring his rope so they could play tug of war. Nugget always won. He would drag Jack on the end of the rope until he let go. They had great fun in the park and Nugget was able to get the exercise he needed. The other dogs in the park would watch Nugget from a distance. If he came near them, they would lie down or roll over with their necks exposed. Jack learned from Dr. Hicks, Nugget's vet, the dogs were cowering to Nugget as a show of respect for his strength. Some of the really tiny dogs just whimpered and ran to hide behind their masters.

In a short while, a man showed up with a Rottweiler and when he let him off the leash, the dog ran right at Jack and Nugget. Nugget moved in front of Jack without even a sound. As the dog got close Nugget jumped and knocked the dog to the ground. Before the dog could do anything Nugget grabbed the Rottweiler by his throat and let out a very deep low growl. The man and the Rottweiler froze as if in a block of ice. Jack walked over to Nugget placing his hand on his shoulder and looked up at the man. The man said he was sorry and that he had never seen anything like that before. He promised not to let his dog loose again if Nugget was there. Jack told him that it was alright. He didn't think the dog would bother them again. As soon as he had spoken, Nugget let go of the Rottweiler and stood back about a foot, watching carefully. The dog remained on the ground on his back for a few seconds and very slowly turned over. He began to creep away from Nugget and went to lie down next to his master. The man put a leash on the Rottweiler and left the park in a big hurry.

When the man left the park all the other masters applauded Jack and Nugget. It seemed that many of them had been in the park before when this particular Rottweiler had shown up. It was a bully of a dog, always jumping on the other dogs in the park. Today it learned a lesson it would never forget. It was a very proud day for Jack. Nugget seemed pretty happy with himself as well. When they got to the gate to go home, Nugget just leaped right over it and waited on the other side for Jack.

Nugget was a very strong jumper. One day Jack's soccer match was delayed. Nugget heard Mira in her backyard. He sailed right over the six foot wall so that he could play with Mira. Mira had a great time and was no longer nervous about Nugget. She was still cautious whenever she was around little jumpy dogs. It seemed that they were more likely to bite, just like the Yorkie that bit her hand. Maybe it was because they were small and everyone else was big. They must get scared.

Nugget got up from his rest spot and walked over to his bowl. He got the soup bone Mira had given him and brought it back to his shady spot under the pomegranate tree to enjoy gnawing it. It helped to clean and sharpen his teeth. He loved getting the marrow out of the bone. The soup bone was a very large bone that Mira had gotten for him at Von's when she was shopping with her Mom.

He was just beginning to enjoy the bone when he heard a strange sound from the front corner of the house. He could also smell a man who did not belong near his den. Nugget shifted his position so that he could keep an eye on the gate. Soon a scruffy looking man appeared. He was creeping slowly around the bushes and looking at the gate. He didn't see Nugget, who was sitting in the shade with the soup bone in his mouth. The man slowly and quietly opened the gate with some sort of tool. When he got inside the gate he closed it carefully and turned around toward the sliding glass doors.

Nugget, with the bone still in his mouth, stood up and walked out of the shade. He just stood there looking at the man who slowly turned to look at Nugget. He made a funny sound and said "nice doggie. Chew your bone." Nugget didn't move for a few seconds then he took one step toward the man and bit his soup bone in half with a loud snap. The man turned pale and slowly began backing up toward the gate. He went out and closed the gate behind him. He took a few steps and thought his troubles were over when Nugget sailed right over the gate. He stared at the man who began yelling as he ran. Nugget followed him until he was out of Jack's yard and watched until he had left the neighborhood. With a doggie smile, Nugget jumped back into the backyard to finish his bone in the shade while waiting for Jack to come home.

Jack came home just as the sun was setting and immediately went to check on Nugget. It was his responsibility to care for Nugget. Dr. Hicks and his parents were very clear about what he needed to do each day. While Nugget may be a wolf dog he thought of himself as a wolf and demanded the respect of a wolf. The dog genes gave him some of his coloring, his happy personality and the slightly webbed toes of a water dog, but the rest was pure wolf.

Jack had looked up wolves on Google and found lots of interesting facts. Wolves evolved about twenty million years ago and are known as the most successful mammals on earth next to man. They are ten times more intelligent than the smartest dogs. They are the largest of the wild canines. Nugget was still a young wolf and yet on his one year checkup Dr. Hicks told Jack he weighed 145 pounds. He also said he would weigh more as he matured. The largest wolf ever recorded was an Alaskan Gray wolf and it weighed 175 pounds. He also found out that wolves have super strong jaws that are double that of the average German Shepard- almost 1,500 pounds of pressure per square inch. They can crush large bones with just a few bites. They can also run thirty five miles per hour for short distances. Wolves usually cover about thirty miles a day hunting for food. Jack knew it was important to exercise Nugget every day by taking him on walks or playing ball.

When Jack got home he ran over to Nugget and gave him a big hug surrounding his shoulders. Nugget was as tall as Jack and certainly outweighed him. Jack talked to Nugget asking about his day and promised him they would spend all weekend together playing. Nugget gave a wag of his tail and licked Jack's face. He couldn't talk to Jack, but he understood what Jack was saying. Jack was also learning to understand some of Nugget's language. It was not human language, but if you were smart and paid attention, which Jack did, you could learn to interpret what Nugget was saying. Wolves communicate by howling, growling, whimpering, barking, eye contact, scent marking and body language. You just had to be observant and remember.

Nugget couldn't tell Jack about the man coming into their yard, but Jack knew from Nugget's body language that he was happy about something. He also saw the almost completely destroyed soup bone.

"Well you must have really liked the bone Mira brought you, Nugget."

Nugget wagged his tale. It was not for the bone so much, rather the mention of Mira. He would enjoy visiting with her too. He loved them both and was happiest when they were all together-just one happy pack. In fact, Mira should be coming home soon and they would all go for a walk before Jack and Mira went to bed. Most of the time Nugget slept in Jack's room, but a couple of times when Jack's family went out of town he got to stay with Mira. Mira's Mom would sneeze a little, but she took something that helped and since Nugget was either out in the backyard or in Mira's room it was okay. He liked Mira's room.

She had a space under her high bed that fitted him perfectly. She even gave him a bunch of old towels that he moved around to make a pillow for his head and the carpet was soft. If Nugget wanted to see Mira he would just stand on his hind legs and put his head next to her. He jumped on her bed once, but there wasn't enough room for both of them and Mira told him to get down. Mira had a funny slight snore when she slept that he found comforting. Jack didn't snore like Mira, but kind of snorted and mumbled while he slept. It was harder to get used to sleeping with Jack.

After Jack fed Nugget and cleaned up the yard, he and Nugget went up to his room. Jack started on his homework while Nugget rested on his dog mattress. It was almost as big as Jack's bed, but that was okay because Jack's room was large. Just as Jack was finishing his homework, Nugget's head popped up and he looked at the door. Jack knew immediately that Nugget had heard Mira coming. Nugget had phenomenal hearing. Phenomenal was a new word he learned in class. It means very good or great in a very impressive way. Jack liked to use it and it fit Nugget perfectly.

They ran down the stairs and met Mira at the front door before she could ring the bell. Jack already had Nugget's leash in his hand and Nugget almost bowled Mira over in his rush to greet her. Mira laughed and gave Nugget a hug as she said "Hi" to Jack. They began walking up the street away from the cul-de-sac. Nugget didn't yank or pull on his leash. It was a comfortable walk up to the corner. They turned left and stayed on the sidewalk while they began a jog. Nugget liked to lope along with them and he could keep going forever. Soon Mira began to slow down to a walk again and she and Jack began to chat about their day. Nothing unusual had happened with either of them - a normal day at school. Jack asked Mira about her birthday party plans.

Mira's birthday was coming up next weekend and Jack was looking forward to the party. Jack had turned nine at Christmas and Mira would be eight at the end of April. Jack was somewhat jealous that she had a birthday that wasn't on a holiday.

"What are you planning this year?"

"Well, I was thinking of having an ice skating party. The rink has a nice room for food and cake and everyone can skate or play some of the video games in the game room. Would you like that?"

"Yes, but you know how I am on skates."

Mira did know. Jack liked to go around fast and usually ended up falling. He was getting better, but he didn't practice much. Still it would be fun with all her friends.

"Mira, do you think we could bring Nugget?" Nugget turned his head around at the mention of his name and gave them both a doggie smile.

"I would love to Jack, but I will have to ask my Mom. I know I've seen some small dogs at the rink in the bleachers. I'm not sure what they'll allow. I promise I'll ask tonight when we get home. You know Jack that we have a day off from school next month."

"We do? What for and when?"

"It's a teacher planning day, so we don't have to go to school. It's on the second Friday of May. I heard my Mom talking about it because the PTA meeting had to be rescheduled."

Jack and Mira had just turned the corner back to their street and were walking silently. They were thinking about what to do with their day off.

"Mira are you thinking what I think you're thinking?"

"Yes, Jack. I'm sure I'm thinking the same thing you are thinking."

"Great. Where should we go this time?"

Just as the words were out of Jack's mouth, a wind rushed around them rattling the trees and blowing loose leaves all over the street. Mira smiled because she knew someone was listening to their conversation. Jack looked around and said.

"I didn't do that Mira. I swear."

"It's okay Jack. We are all excited about traveling again. Look even Nugget seems excited."

Nugget was prancing about in a sort of doggie dance as they reached Jack's house and said goodbye. Mira gave Nugget another hug and headed for her house. "I'll let you know what my Mom says about Nugget."

"Mom, I'm home from our walk."

"Great, Kiddo. How was it? How is Nugget?"

"Mom, speaking of Nugget, can he come to my birthday party?"

Well, now. I haven't thought about that. I don't see why not since we are having a private party. We rented out the entire rink for three hours. I'll call the rink tomorrow and make sure it's okay."

"Thanks Mom. That's great."

Stephen Meritt

Chapter 2

Jack had just gotten into his superman PJs when he heard the now familiar squawk of his walkie talkie unit.

"Hi Mira. What did your Mom say? Over."

"She said Nugget could come as far as she was concerned. She would need to okay it with the rink, but since it's a private party she thought it would be fine. Over."

"Phenomenal! I'll see you in school tomorrow and at the party on Saturday. Goodnight. Over and out."

"Goodnight. Out."

Mira got into her PJs and was lying in bed with a book, but she really wasn't able to concentrate. So many thoughts were running through her head. Tomorrow was Friday and school would be fine, but Saturday was coming and all she could think about was her party. She had new ice skating clothes that would be perfect. Her Grandparents were arriving tomorrow too. They always came for her birthday parties. Of course, they knew about Nugget, but had not met him yet. She hoped they would love him too.

She was not at all sure of what presents she would get. With Nugget's arrival in their lives, she hadn't been thinking about much else. What about traveling again? Where would they go? She knew they would take Nugget, but where? There was so much on her mind right now that she didn't think she would be able to fall asleep at all as she drifted off.

Friday afternoon when school ended, Mira was met by her Mom and Grandma Sandi and Grandpa Steve. They were her Mom's parents. She got big hugs from both. Grandpa Steve apologized for going to lunch at Jerry's without her. He said he spoke to her other Grandmother, Elda. She had arrived from Baltimore earlier and was at her Uncle's house. She would see her tomorrow. Grandma Sandi and Grandpa Steve were staying at Mira's house.

"I am going to have an ice skating party tomorrow. Will you skate, Grandpa?"

"Nope. My ice skating days are over. I still remember how, but I don't bounce as well anymore. Besides, I don't want to break the ice. I'll be happy watching you and your friends skate and eating cake, of course."

Grandpa Steve used to be a good skater and taught her Mom how to skate when she was a kid. Now that he has turned seventy, he didn't want to be on the ice, at least not on skates.

"Guess what, Grandpa? Mom said I can bring Nugget to the party. Isn't that great?"

"Absolutely, we are looking forward to meeting Nugget when we get home. Will you introduce us? I really miss having a dog."

Grandpa Steve loved dogs, more than Grandma Sandi. He grew up with dogs and still had a big photo of his favorite hunting dog on point over his desk. He was a Pointer named Damnit. Mira always giggled when she heard that name. She wasn't supposed to use curse words even though she knew a few from her classmates who had older brothers or sisters. So she liked the opportunity to say Damnit. She once asked Grandpa Steve how Damnit got his name. He said when he got Damnit from a veterinarian, he was in college. College kids would occasionally use curse words. It seemed that every time they would say damn it, the pup would come running, so everyone just started calling him Damnit. He said it caused him to get funny looks from his neighbors when he went outside to call the dog, DAMNIT, come here boy.

They all piled into her Mom's car and headed for the frozen yogurt shop on the way home. It was Grandpa Steve's suggestion for an after school treat. The shop was self-serve. Mira loved to sample the different flavors and add candy sprinkles to the one she selected. They all enjoyed the frozen yogurt and then headed home. Nugget heard them drive up and didn't wait in Jack's yard. He jumped right over the gate as they were getting out of the car.

"OH My! Now that's what I call a dog." Said Grandpa Steve. "Mira, go bring him to us, please."

Grandpa Steve got down on one knee and lowered his head while putting his hand out for Nugget to sniff. Nugget slowly sniffed all around Grandpa Steve and finally licked his hand. Nugget seemed to know that he was part of Mira's pack. Grandpa Steve rubbed Nugget's head and ears which Nugget loved. Then they wrestled a little and Nugget ended up running all around the yard playing with Grandpa Steve. Jack arrived and everyone said hello. Nugget gave Jack a lick and they all parted so that Mira's grandparents could unpack.

"I'll see you tomorrow at the party with Nugget." Jack said as he walked to his front door. Mira waved and Nugget wagged.

Mira and her Grandparents talked while they unpacked. They had brought her some new clothes because Grandma Sandi always found something for her when she went shopping. Grandma Sandi had great taste in clothes. She always brought pretty things. Grandpa Steve had picked out a new pair of size two New Balance hiking boots. It was perfect for her to use on her next adventure with Jack. She would begin wearing them right away so they would be broken in for her next trip. Grandpa Steve knew about the traveling tornado. When Mira and Jack had gone to Florida to go fishing with him, they had arrived while he was working on the lawn. He was really cool about it and kept their secret. Her Mom suspected, but didn't say anything.

Mira's Mom had ordered Chinese takeout for dinner from one of their favorite restaurants called Yang Chow. Mira loved their slippery shrimp and Grandpa Steve loved their spicy won ton soup. While her Dad and Grandpa Steve went to pick up dinner, she and Grandma Sandi went over some of her school work. They knocked out her homework so she could spend the rest of the weekend playing with everyone. Grandma Sandi was a retired specialist who specialized in teaching English to elementary school children who came from other countries. She didn't have her own classroom, but went around from school to school helping the teachers. She always had funny stories to tell about her teachers and the students. She knew exactly what Mira was doing in school. Mira loved learning what other school children were doing.

After dinner was cleaned up, Mira went off to get ready for bed while her Parents and Grandparents talked and put together party favors. She had her shower, put on her PJs and read a story to her Grandparents. They used to read her stories when she was younger and now she enjoyed reading stories to them. They didn't finish a whole book; it would've taken too long. They just read a few chapters. It helped get her ready for bed. Grandpa Steve insisted on giving her a bouncy tuck which he called a gorilla tuck. It always made her giggle. Tomorrow was going to be great fun.

Just as Grandpa Steve closed the door to her room, she heard the squawk of her walkie talkie. She hopped out of bed to grab it before her parents heard the noise.

"Hi Jack. What's up? Over."

"I just wanted to say goodnight. I'll see you at the party with Nugget. He has a surprise for you. Over."

"Really, what? Over."

"Forget it. I am not telling. You'll see tomorrow. Night. Over and out."

"Out."

What in the world was Jack up to? This was Nugget's first outing to a skating rink and the first time many of her friends would meet him. She hoped everything would go well for Nugget's sake. All sorts of things were going through her mind as she drifted off to sleep.

Chapter 3

The birthday party day arrived and everyone, except Mira's Dad, piled into her Mom's SUV for the drive to the ice rink. The mood was festive and hectic with all the favors in the way back. The cake and her Dad were coming in his car because there wasn't room for everything in the SUV.

The rink had a nice enclosed room set up for them complete with balloons and a banner that said HAPPY BIRTHDAY MIRA. Her Mom had blue table clothes on the tables and began setting out the favors. Her Grandparents also helped set things up as Mira went to put on her skates. The first of her friends were arriving. Some of the parents stayed to watch and help out. Her friend Sadie came in with her two younger twin sisters, Ruby and Addie. Sadie had the same birthday as Mira and her party was going to be tomorrow. This was going to be a party weekend. Next came her first cousins, Oscar and

Jacob, they would both be turning twelve this year. Her second cousin Ryan would also be coming, he was fifteen. Mira had more cousins, but they couldn't come because they're off in college. More friends arrived in a big group. There was Chloe, Riley, Zack, Noah, Campbell, Joseph, Madison, Alexandra, Ashley and Isabella,

Then the door opened and in came Jack with Nugget at his side. Nugget was wearing a blue and gold bandana with the initial N on the broad part of the cloth. It must have been specially made because it just fit Nugget, but was big enough to be a cape if Jack wore it. Nugget had a rope handle in his mouth which allowed him to carry a large gift box. Everyone stopped to stare. They'd all heard about Nugget, but they didn't pay much attention until they saw him in person. He was huge. He stood taller than most of the children while on all fours. Several people took his picture. Nugget handled himself like a pro. He sat quietly and let the children touch and pet him all the while holding the present in his mouth.

Mira gave Jack a big hug and told him that the outfit for Nugget was pure genius. It made him look like a well-mannered big dog and effectively hid his wolf looks. She was so proud of both Jack and

Nugget. She gave Nugget a hug and an ear scratch and he dropped the box at her feet. Mira knelt down and hugged him around his neck before picking up the gift.

"Thank you, Jack. Bringing Nugget was the best present all by itself. I'll put this with the other presents to open later."

"You're welcome, Mira. I am so happy you were able to let Nugget come. I can't wait until he sees the ice."

They all walked together to the shoe station so Jack could get some skates. Nugget just watched and crooked his head from one side to the other. He sniffed at the skates that made Jack and Mira taller. He walked over to the ice rink and carefully smelled the edge. He had never seen a pond with ice on it before. He hadn't lived through a cold winter in the mountains yet so he wasn't too sure what to do about the ice.

Once Mira and Jack skated onto the ice a few feet, Nugget decided he would follow. Of course, everyone was watching as he stepped on the ice and his paws went right out from under him. He slid a few feet on his belly and tried to get up. His feet were scrambling in all directions until he sat down and pulled his two front feet together. Once he found a stable position he began to slowly place his feet on the ice. In a moment, he was able to stand without falling. A minute later he could walk on the ice and he began to pick up a little speed. He followed Jack and Mira around on the ice, slipping once in a while. Everyone was amazed at how quickly Nugget seemed to master this new experience.

"I told you he was smart." Said Jack. "He can handle anything."

"I know Jack. He is the best dog ever. We're so lucky."

They led Nugget to the entrance and let him out of the gate. He watched as they began skating around the oval. He could see them through the plexiglas wall. Once they went around he started to follow them. He could easily trot around the outside of the oval while they skated inside. He liked that game and soon they were going faster and faster. It was quite a show. Nugget could easily outrun the skaters and did so frequently and then he'd stop to allow them to catch up. As soon as they did, he would take off again. It was a game he liked and never seemed to tire. Eventually they all stopped skating when it was time for food and cake.

Jack was smart enough to bring along some special food for Nugget while the kids ate pizzas. A few kids slipped Nugget some pizza which he thoroughly enjoyed. You might say he wolfed it right down. As the party wound down and the kids and their parents began to leave, they all said goodbye to Nugget who had stationed himself at the door. It may have been Mira's birthday, but Nugget was definitely the hit of the party. Jack's parents and Sadie's parents all stayed to help clean up and take the presents out to the car. Mira would open them all at home so she could make a list for the thank you notes. Sadie told her she could bring Nugget to her party tomorrow if she wanted. Sadie had two dogs of her own, but they didn't behave like Nugget. Mira thanked her for the invitation, but said Nugget would be resting tomorrow.

Everyone made it home safe and sound. Jack and Nugget waved and wagged as they went to his house. Mira helped carry all the presents into her family room, where her parents and grandparents gathered. Grandma Elda had joined them, but would have to go back to Mira's Uncle's house later. Mira's house didn't have enough room for both sets of Grandparents to sleep. Mira thought maybe one day they would get a bigger house. She had heard her Parents talking about it, but that would mean moving away from Jack and Nugget and she really didn't want that now. She realized that she was perfectly happy right now with things just as they were. The saying "remember what you wished for" popped into her mind.

She began opening her presents and her Mom wrote down what each present was and who had given it to her. Her Grandma Sandi was sitting on the floor right next to her taking away the trash. Everyone else watched and oohed as each present was opened. Most were clothes and a few games. The two biggest surprises were a bigger bike from her Parents and a pair of professional ice skates in the box Nugget had carried from Jack. They were white with tiny embroidered initials MS in blue on the outer flaps. Mira looked over at her Mom and her Mother just nodded. She had given Jack's parents Mira's shoe size.

After all the presents were opened and put away, everyone had takeout for dinner. It was Italian food. Grandma Elda was from a large Italian family and she said the food was exceptionally good. After dinner everyone sat around telling stories and talking about all sorts of things. Grandpa Steve mentioned that the food was almost as good as the food they had when they visited Italy. It was then that her Mom told everyone about the food she had in a small Italian café right across from the Coliseum in Rome. Mira asked her Mom when was she in Rome? Mira's Mom travels a lot for her work, but never mentioned Rome.

"When I was sixteen years old, I was in the Latin Club in my high school and we had a summer trip to Rome. We got to see all the ancient ruins of the Roman Empire. Rome was the capital of the Roman Empire and it's now the capital of Italy. They used to speak Latin. Now they speak Italian. It is similar to the Spanish you're learning in school."

"Can I take Latin?"

"It will be offered when you get to high school or maybe even junior high. If you still want to take it you may."

Mira yawned and told everyone she was ready to go to bed. She hugged Grandma Elda and said she would see her next week, since she would be staying for another two weeks. Grandma Sandi and Grandpa Steve were leaving early in the morning before she even got up because Grandpa Steve had patients scheduled on Monday. She gave them each a long hug and kisses. She thanked them again for the presents and for coming all the way to California for her party. She said she would see them again when she came to their house for the Fourth of July.

Mira washed up and got into her PJs and immediately squawked Jack on the walkie talkie. She heard Jack mumble something, but couldn't understand him.

"Jack, are you there? Over."

"Yes, I was just falling asleep. What's up? Over."

"I know where we are going on our next adventure. Over."

"WHAT, WHERE? Over."

"Rome." Over."

"Why Rome? You do mean Rome? The one in Italy? Over."

"Yes. I will explain the whole thing to you next week in school. Okay? Over.

"I guess. Goodnight. Over and out."

"Goodnight. Out."

Stephen Meritt

Chapter 4

Monday morning in school was uneventful that is if you could call Jack looking at Mira every chance he got uneventful. He even glanced out the window from his class to hers. It made Mira smile to know Jack was so gaga about the trip to Rome. She knew she would be bombarded with questions the minute the lunch bell rang and she was right. Jack ran out of class as soon as he could with his lunch box in his hand and went straight to Mira's class. He waited impatiently outside her classroom door for everyone to file out. Of course, Mira was near the end of the line since she wasn't in a particular hurry. Poor Jack was bouncing from one foot to the other, like he had to go to the bathroom. Mira just couldn't help herself. She began laughing.

"Okay, cut it out Mira. Tell me what's happening. I want to know everything. Tell me."

"Take it easy Jack. I'll tell you in the lunch room."

"Why can't you just tell me now?"

"Be patient Jack, let's sit down."

So Jack and Mira made the short walk to the lunchroom and found a table near the window. Luckily, they were the only ones at the table for the time being. Jack didn't even open his lunch box, but watched Mira open hers. As she began to take out her lunch, Jack made a strangling sound and looked at her as if he was going to burst.

"MIRA!"

"Okay Jack, calm down."

Jack took a deep breath and sat back in his seat. Mira began to tell him the story of her Mom's teenage trip to Rome with her Latin Club. She told him about the old ruins and the coliseum where the gladiators fought. She even told him about the café across the street. She could see the excitement in

Jack's face as soon as she mentioned gladiators. She knew at that moment he was hooked on Rome. Yes, this was going to be a memorable trip. This trip just felt right.

"So when can we begin planning?"

"We'll work on it this weekend, when we find the time. This time will be different because of the time changes."

"What'd you mean?"

"Jack, you know about time zones. We studied it in geography, remember."

Jack slapped his hand on his head. "Oh man, I didn't think of that. How are we going to handle that?"

"Don't worry; I'll come up with something. Just give me some time."

"Okay, Mira. Cool."

Jack was smiling now as he opened his lunch box. "Nuts, Mom gave me bologna again. She gave me boloney yesterday. Want to trade?"

"You know we aren't supposed to trade? I have a cold grilled cheese on marble rye."

"Pleeeease, no one is looking. Here, enjoy the bologna. It's Oscar Meyer."

Jack was smiling from ear to ear as he traded sandwiches with Mira. Mira didn't mind. She really liked the grilled cheese even cold, but Jack was her best friend and traveling companion. How could she not trade? Besides, she liked bologna too. The rest of the day went well and after school Mira had soccer practice with a professional coach. The extra practice was for kids in her age group that wanted extra coaching to improve their game skills. She went twice a week and it seemed to be working. At her last game she scored two goals and had one assist.

She did her homework before dinner and after dinner watched a movie on Netflix with her parents. As she was getting ready for bed and looking in her closet for what she wanted to wear to school tomorrow, she spotted her sleeping bag rolled up neatly in the corner near the door. All of a sudden an idea popped into her head. She thought she had a way to handle the time zone change for their trip. She would have to do some brief research and a little simple math, but that was not a problem.

Before getting in bed, she went into her Dad's office and asked him about time zones that they studied in school. He said that she must already know about them since her Grandparents live on the east coast. She knew it was three hours later on the east coast than where they lived on the west coast. He typed a few keys on his computer and all the time zones popped up on the monitor. She could see that Rome was nine hours ahead of LA. She listened to her Dad explain the zones and the date line with only half an ear as she was thinking about the trip. She thanked her Dad and kissed him goodnight.

"Would you like a tuck, Pumpkin?"

"Sure Dad. That would be great."

Her Dad got up and followed her into her

room and watched as she turned out the light and climbed up the ladder. He took her blanket and tucked her in on both sides.

"You know, Pumpkin, I kind of miss reading you bedtime stories. Now you read your own books. I know you read by flash light sometimes when you are supposed to be sleeping."

"How did you know that?"

"Now come on, you know I'm magical."

"DAD!"

"Okay, I saw the light under your door one night. It was moving around, so I knew it was your flash light. It's okay with your Mom and me if you read in bed, but remember you need as much rest as possible for school and all your after school activities."

"Okay, Dad. Thanks, I'll keep my reading short. Will you read me my old favorite story tonight? You know the one."

"Sure, Pumpkin.   Here you go. Goodnight Moon…"

When he finished the short Goodnight Moon story, He reached over and gave Mira another kiss.

Oh, and tell Jack goodnight for me too."

"DAD!"

"Gotcha. Remember, I was a pretty smart kid myself once."

He was laughing as he went out, closing Mira's door behind him. She immediately knew that he had overheard them talking on the walkie talkie. She would have to be more careful from now on. Her parents were pretty sharp. She reached over and snagged the yellow walkie talkie unit from where she had hung it on the side of her bed. She pressed the call button and waited for Jack to answer. It didn't take too long.

"Hi Mira, what's up. Over."

"I figured it out. Over."

"Figured what out? Over."

"Jack! You know. I can't talk here. I don't have a room upstairs and my dad has heard me talking to you. He even told me to tell you goodnight. See you in school. Goodnight and rub Nugget for me. Over and out."

"Will do. Goodnight. Out."

Tuesday turned out to be a cool and misty day which was a little different. It is usually cool in the mornings, but not misty. Some sort of shift in the wind occured. As soon as she thought of wind, Mariah came to her mind and she immediately heard a giggle.

"Yes, I did it, Little One. Are we about ready to take another trip?"

"Yes," Mira thought. "We are beginning to plan one soon. Will that be okay with you?"

"Certainly, I enjoy our time together. I am ready whenever you are. Don't worry about rain clothes today. The sun is about to shine."

Mira got dressed in her regular clothes for school and walked into the kitchen for breakfast. Her Mom was having coffee and finishing up making her lunch. In the lunch box was an apple and some grapes, and a grape jelly sandwich on white bread.

"Hi Kiddo, how about having an Eggo waffle for breakfast? Drink your smoothie."

As Mira began drinking her smoothie, her Mom put two Eggo waffles in the toaster oven. She went back to her coffee and looked out the window at the misty blowing weather.

"You might want to put on a different outfit today with this weather."

"It's okay Mom the sun will come out."

"Predicting the weather now, Kiddo?"

"Yep."

The toaster oven rang and her Mom took the waffles out and put them on a plate. She buttered them lightly and let Mira pour the maple syrup. After breakfast, Mira brushed her teeth and finished getting ready for school. They went to the front door where Mira put on her shoes and said goodbye to her Dad who was already on his computer. Her Mom grabbed her purse and slipped into her shoes while opening the door. She had also put on a rain slicker. She opened the door into a bright sunny morning.

"Well I'll be... [Pause] "

Mira was almost sure her Mom was about to say a bad word, but she caught herself just in time. She turned around and looked at Mira, who just smiled a slight little smile and did a little curtsey.

"You know don't you, Mira Summers, that one of these days, I am going to figure out what's going on here don't you?"

Mira just smiled and said.

"I love you Mom. We're going to be late for school."

Chapter 5

They made it to school in the nick of time. The Flag ceremony was about to start. Mira saw Jack who nodded to her and mouthed lunch. Mira nodded back and after the flag had been raised went to her classroom.

The lunch bell rang and Mira grabbed her lunch box and headed over to the lunch room. Jack was already sitting at a table waiting for her. Just as Mira sat down a couple of fifth grade boys walked by and made comments about Jack's girlfriend. Jack started to get up, but Mira put her hand on his arm.

"Forget those jerks. They don't have anything better to do with their time. Besides, I am your friend and a girl."

"I know Mira, but they are always talking

about me. They have been at it ever since my team beat theirs in our last match."

"Think of it this way, they know you are better than they are, so they jerk you around. Ignore them. You know that they know that you are the best."

Jack seemed to swell a little and told Mira "Thanks."

Now tell me what you figured out about how to handle the time zones."

"Okay. Here's what we do. The planning day is on a Friday, so we tell our parents a few days before the teacher planning day that we want to camp out in your back yard on that Thursday night. You know we'll have a tent, sleeping bags, backpacks with all our gear and Nugget too. Then we wait until late in the evening, around ten o'clock to travel so that we arrive in the early morning in Italy. There is a nine hour difference, so 10:00 in the evening will get us there at 7:00 in the morning."

"Brilliant, but what about our parents? Won't they wonder about us or check on us?"

"Well, I think we need to have your Mom or Dad help us set up the tent with the sleeping bags and a camp light. When we turn out the light, they'll figure we've gone to sleep, but we will actually be ready to leave. They know we will be okay with Nugget around. I don't know any other way to do it. Do you have any ideas?"

"Nope, I think it might work. I have a little two person igloo tent and a Coleman lantern that uses batteries. We can bring snacks and drinks so there is no reason to go in the house or have my parents come out."

"Great, we just have to be sure to get back before your parents get up in the morning and come to check on us."

"Okay. We have a plan. We are going to Italy on the second Friday in May. That's only nine days away which is plenty of time to get everything ready."

Mira and Jack opened their lunch boxes.

"Bologna again." said Jack as looked over at Mira.

Mira took out her Jelly sandwich and said "nope, don't even think about it, Jack."

The rest of the day went smoothly and after school Jack headed to soccer while Mira went to skating practice. She wanted to try learning sit spins and the teacher promised to show her some tricks. The week went well with Mira getting an A on her math test. Jack got an A too, so it was going to be a nice weekend for planning. Saturday after they had both finished their soccer games. Mira called Jack on the walkie talkie and asked him if she could come over with her backpack. Jack said sure, but didn't sound too happy.

"What's bothering you Jack? Over."

"We lost our game today. Over."

"Forget it; you'll get them next time. Think

about the trip. Over and out."

"Okay, you're right, come on over. Out."

Mira gathered her backpack and told her Mom that she was heading over to Jack's to play with Nugget. Her Mom told her she would call over to Jack's when she had firmed up the evening's plans. Mira went out the front door and over to Jack's house. A stiff breeze blew her pony tail around her head.

"Okay, Mariah. We are planning to travel with you very soon."

Mira heard a giggle just as she reached Jack's door. She could hear Nugget on the other side. A few seconds later Jack opened the door and Mira was almost knocked over by Nugget's greeting. He licked her face in a big wet doggie kiss. Jack laughed at her as she wiped her face on her sleeve.

"Hi, Nugget. I love you too."

"Come on in, Mira. Let's go to my room and

make sure the backpacks are together."

They ran up the stairs with Nugget in the lead. As they walked into Jack's room, Mira looked around in awe. Jack's room was neat and clean. Everything was picked up and in its place. Jack saw Mira's expression and turned slightly red in the face.

"Jack today's not Sunday and your room is clean."

"I know. With Nugget in the room all the time I had to start keeping it straight or he would move everything around. My Mom thinks it's one of the best things about our getting Nugget."

Mira couldn't help but smile and then Jack did too as he reached for his backpack. They sat on the floor in the middle of the room and emptied their packs. Nugget kept poking his head into the backpacks looking to see if there was more food. Maybe even some Vienna Sausages. Mira and Jack laughed when one pack got caught on his head and he was swinging it back and forth to get it off. It fell on the floor and Nugget just sat and looked at them with his doggie smile.

"Okay Jack, I still have the flash light, the ten dollars, the compass, the whistle and the rope. I don't have any food. What about you?"

"I have my flash light, the compass and my pocket knife. I don't have any food either. Do we need food?"

"Hum, good question. If we are going to be in Rome we shouldn't need to carry any food, except maybe a doggie snack for Nugget."

"I can put some milk bones in my pack. Do we need clothes, Mira?"

"No. I shouldn't think so, as far as weather is concerned. It will be warm, but then again if something happened we might need a change."

"Okay, I'll put a pair of jeans in and a shirt. You'll have to bring your extra clothes over next time or on Thursday. Have you asked your parents about the camp out yet?"

"No. I'll ask my Mom tomorrow. If she says

yes my Dad will be fine with it. If I ask Dad he'll just tell me to ask Mom."

"It's the same here, but if it's okay with you let's ask my Mom together. She is more likely to agree with you next to me."

"Okay, when?"

"Come on, let's do it now."

Jack jumped up and pulled Mira up. Nugget followed them downstairs as Jack hollered "MOM!"

"I'm in the den, Jack"

Jack, Mira and Nugget went through the great room and into the den which was on the other side of the room opposite the kitchen. Jack's Mom was sitting in the lounge chair reading a magazine with the TV on mute.

"Oh, hi Mira, I didn't realize you were here darling. How are you?"

"Fine, thank you Mrs. Jones."

"Mom, you know that we are out of school on Friday for the teacher's planning day, right?"

"Yes, dear."

"Well, can Mira and I camp out with a tent in our backyard Thursday night?"

"Well, I don't see why not. Mira what did your Mom say?"

"I haven't asked her yet. We're going over to ask her after we asked you."

"Okay. Well, I 'll tell you what, it's okay with me if it's okay with your Mom."

"Great. Thanks Mom."

Jack, Mira and Nugget headed out to Mira's house at a trot, trying not to be too crazy so as to make Jack's Mom wonder about the whole project.

Jack even remembered not to slam the door. Nugget darted after a squirrel in the yard and circled back to Mira when the squirrel ran around the side of a tree. The squirrel was very upset and sat up in a branch making lots of funny noises.

They dropped their shoes inside Mira's front door and found Mira's Mom in the office working on her computer.

"Hi Kiddo. Jack. Nugget. How was your week?"

"Fine. Thank you."

"Mom, Jack asked me to camp out with him in a tent in his backyard on Thursday night. Friday is the teacher's planning day and we don't have school. His Mom said it's okay with her if it's okay with you. May I, please?"

"Sure, why not. We don't have any plans and if you are going to be at Jack's house with his parents' home, your Dad and I might eat out and take in a movie. I'll call your Mom, Jack, and confirm it."

"Thanks, Mrs. Summers."

"Thanks Mom." Mira gave her Mom a hug. "We are going back over to Jack's to plan and I want to see his tent."

"Okay, Kiddo. Be back in an hour. Please."

Mira and Jack put their shoes back on and went back out the front door. The squirrel was still chattering in the tree. He was not happy. Nugget didn't pay him any attention as they all ran back to Jack's house. Once again they shed their shoes and Jack ran into the den and told his Mom that Mrs. Summers said it was okay and that they might go out to dinner and a movie.

"Oh, I should have thought of that myself. Oh, well, next time." Just as she finished talking the phone rang and the TV ID'd the caller as Mrs. Summers. "Okay, you kids run along while I talk to Mira's Mom.

Jack and Mira went around the corner and stopped to eavesdrop on the conversation. Of course, they could only hear one side of the conversation. They heard Jack's Mom say:

"Hi Gray, (Mira's Mom's name is Grayson, but all her friends call her Gray) are you okay with Mira and Jack camping out in our backyard? Nugget will be with them and we will be home. We didn't have any plans. I heard you might go out on a date night with your husband to a real movie. We need to do that too one day. I am tired of seeing kid flicks. Listen, Mira can come over after school and eat with us so you needn't worry about her dinner. Just go out and enjoy the evening. Great, we'll plan it one day soon. The kids will be fine. Okay, talk to you later. Bye."

Mira and Jack smiled and gave each other quiet high fives and walked quietly around the great room and up the stairs with Nugget on their heels. Once in Jack's room they laughed and sat down with a sigh. The tricky part was over now all they had to do was plan the trip.

"So we know what to take, but do you know where we need to go when we get there?

Mira thought about it a minute and said.

"We'll ask Mm, err, the tornado, to take us to a park closest to the coliseum. It is supposed to be in the middle of the city. I am sure there will be signs or a tourist map. Italian is a lot like Spanish and we know some Spanish. A lot of people speak English so I don't think we'll have a problem. It will be early in the morning on a weekday and before the crowds. What do you think?"

"I think it is perfect. This is going to be a great trip."

Jack walked Mira back downstairs to where they had dropped her shoes. Nugget gave her a nudge in the back and sniffed at her neck which was just nose high. Mira laughed and turn around to give Nugget a big hug.

"Jack, remember to put Nugget's leash and neck bandana in your backpack. We will need it for walking around in Rome. We don't need to break any laws."

"Good thinking. I'll do it right now. I have a spare leash. Bye Mira."

"Bye, Jack, Bye Nugget."

Mira went home and after removing her shoes found her Mom in the kitchen.

"Thanks Mom. It'll be fun and we'll be good."

"I know, Kiddo. We trust you and Jack and especially Nugget. The Joneses have asked you to dinner that night, so Dad and I can have an adult night. Is that okay with you?"

"Sure. Mom."

Chapter 6

Thursday had arrived at last. Jack didn't think the week would ever end. It was as bad as waiting for Christmas. Mira felt the same way and had told him so at lunch that day as they traded sandwiches again. Jack got home from school and soccer practice and raced up to his room to get out the camping gear. The tent was stored on the top shelf of his closet. It is a modern igloo type of tent that didn't require any ropes. Instead it had several long aluminum poles that folded up with elastic cording. Once opened each pole was 10 feet long.

The tent material was a double layer of nylon with long loops on the outside. It also had a floor and the whole thing was waterproof. The zipper door was round and really cool. To put it up you simply connected the poles and slid them through the loops. They supported the tent like a geodesic dome. Even niftier was that it rolled up into a very small oblong pack that would fit in most backpacks.

Stephen Meritt

After pulling out the tent, Jack fought a hard battle to pull out his sleeping bag which was stuffed on the side shelf. Once out he unrolled it and found a few left over leaves from his last camping trip. When Nugget sniffed it and sneezed he definitely knew it needed airing out. He slung it over his shoulder and took it downstairs to the backyard. He unzipped the bag and shook it out really hard and left it to air on the patio table. Nugget followed him around and up and down as Jack ran about looking for his lantern. He finally found it in the garage and the batteries were dead. He needed a Phillips head screw driver to open the battery compartment which was on the bottom. After removing the four screws he found that he needed four D batteries, just what he didn't have in the house.

Jack ran back to his room and squawked Mira.

"Hi Jack. Are you getting ready? Over."

"Yeah, but the batteries were dead in the lantern. Do you have any D cells? The big round ones. Over"

58

"Hold a sec. Over. I found six in our battery drawer. Over."

"Great, we need four. Bring them over when you come, okay. Over."

"Will do. Over and out."

"Out."

Jack went back to his room to finish putting his backpack in order. Meanwhile, Mira was relaxing reading a book. She had put her backpack in order days ago. All she needed to do was grab it and head over to Jack's. Dinner was to be at six o'clock and it was just 5:30. Her Mom was in the shower getting ready to go out to dinner and a movie with her Dad. Her Dad was still on the computer, since he didn't need as much time to get ready. Mira couldn't help but smile at how well this plan had worked out so far. She and Jack would camp out and when everyone else was asleep, around 10:00, they would call Mariah and take off for Rome. When they got to Rome it would be 7:00 in the morning. It would be perfect to start a day of sightseeing she thought.

A few minutes before she was supposed to go over to Jack's, her Mom came into her room and gave her a kiss.

"Remember to be good, and mind your manners. And by the way, be careful and try to stay out of trouble. I know you and Jack are up to something. We will be home late maybe around midnight. If you need us just call our cells. Okay?"

"Okay, Mom. We'll be good. I love you."

"Scoot then Kiddo. Jack is waiting."

Mira picked up her backpack, sleeping bag and her book as she went to the front door to put on her jogging shoes. Her Dad called her into his office while she was tying her shoes.

"Hey, Pumpkin Head. Are you already for your big adventure?"

Mira's heart started pounding. She practically stammered her first word. "Wwwhat Dad?"

"You know your camping adventure with Jack. What did you think I was talking about?" There was a look in his eye just like her Mom had when they got back from Norway.

"Oh, sorry Dad. I guess I was confused for a moment. I was tying my shoes when you called me.

"That's alright Pumpkin Butt. I just wanted to tell you to have fun. I want to hear all about it in the morning. I love you."

"Thanks Dad, I love you too."

Mira went back to the door, picked up her backpack and slung it over her left shoulder. She yelled bye and went out to a beautiful late afternoon. She stopped briefly to look around. The sun was heading down and the sky was a beautiful shade of blue with a few scattered clouds. It was perfect.

Nugget came bounding around the flower bed and practically knocked her down.

"Whoa boy. We will be together all night.

Come on, don't lick my face. Down boy."

Nugget finally settled down and began sniffing the flower bed. Then he ran over to the tree and looked up for the squirrel who was nowhere to be seen. Disappointed, Nugget wet down the base of the tree and bounced back over to Jack who was standing in his front door.

"Hi Mira. We're having pizza for dinner from the California Pizza Kitchen. Dad should be here any minute. He was picking them up on his way home from the office. Did you remember the batteries?"

"Great, I love pizza. I have the batteries in my backpack."

They went into the house with Nugget running around in small circles ahead of them. He knew something was up and he was ready. Jack took the batteries from Mira as she set her backpack and sleeping bag on the patio. There was no need to take it to Jack's room. After all, they would just have to bring it down again. Jack was working on the lantern so Mira went into the kitchen. Mrs. Jones was fixing a salad to go with the pizza.

"Hi, Mrs. Jones. Can I help you with anything?"

"Hi Sweetie. Yes, that's so nice of you. Take the salad bowls out to the table, please. We are going to eat on the patio tonight. Then come back and I'll let you help with the dressing. Where's Jack?"

"He's putting new batteries in the lantern."

"I swear that boy leaves everything to the last minute."

Mira carried the four salad bowls out and set them on the large patio table. The umbrella was up and she noticed a slight breeze. She went back to the kitchen and Mrs. Jones gave her a bowl with several spices in the bottom.

"Pour the olive oil over the spices and stir it around until it is well mixed. The oil is in the measuring cup on your right."

Mira poured the olive oil over the spices being careful not to spill any. She took the wooden mixing spoon and stirred the oil and spices together until she had a paste. Mrs. Jones came over and added just a little more olive oil and then thick balsamic vinegar to the mixture. She told Mira to stir it again for a minute and then tasted a little bit from the spoon.

"Perfect Mira. You'd make a good sous chef."

"What's a sous chef?"

"That is someone that is the second in command of the kitchen. They are responsible for making sure everything the chef needs is ready."

"Thanks, Mrs. Jones."

"Okay, Sweetie, run along and see what trouble Jack has gotten into."

Mira got to the porch just as Jack finished closing up the battery compartment of the lantern. Mr. Jones was just coming in the garage door with three big pizza boxes.

"Give me a hand Jack."

"Sure Dad."

Jack took the pizza boxes straight out to the patio table while his Dad grabbed his briefcase and a file folder. Apparently, he had planned on doing some work this evening after dinner. Jack had told Mira that he often brought case work home with him. He said Hi to Mira as he headed into his office to set things down.

By 6:30 everyone was seated at the patio table passing around the salad and pizza. One pizza had pepperoni, one was veggie and one was a mix of everything. It was called a kitchen sink. Mira had three slices, one of each. Jack had four slices of the pepperoni. Mr. Jones ate only the Kitchen sink and Mrs. Jones chose the veggie. Nugget ate everything that touched the floor.

By 7:30 dinner was over and cleaned up. Mr. Jones asked Jack if he needed any help with the tent.

"No thanks. I already set it up in the side yard, not too far from the pool."

"Good, oh by the way, no swimming without one of us watching. That means no swimming after we go to bed. Understand?"

"Yes sir" said Jack and Mira together.

Jack and Mira got their backpacks and sleeping bags and walked over to the tent. Jack unzipped the door and said "Ta Da." Mira crawled in and unrolled her sleeping bag on one side. Jack did the same with his on the other side. Nugget walked in and filled up the whole tent. His tail was swatting Jack's head while Mira was fighting off another doggie kiss. Mira was laughing hysterically.

"Out, Nugget", said Jack and peace returned to the tent. They got out the lantern, turned it on and hung it on a convenient snap at the center of the dome.

"Let's check our backpacks."

"We really don't need much this time, Jack. We aren't going to the wilds. We have some clothes and the canteens. We also have the Maglites. We shouldn't need compasses, but they're in there already. Certainly no rope will be necessary. The walkie talkie could come in handy. Can you think of anything else?"

"What about snacks?"

"We will be in a city and we have money to buy snacks. You still have the ten dollars don't' you?

"Yes. So I guess we are set. All we have to do now is wait until time to leave. What should we do?"

"I brought a book to read."

"Boooring."

"Okay, what do you want to do?"

"Let's play cards. Do you know how to play Blackjack?"

"Sure."

Jack jumped up and went to get the cards while Mira read her book. When Jack returned he said his Dad would be going to bed early because he had to meet a client at the office early before going to court. His Mom usually reads at night and is in bed around 9:30.

"They are going to leave the downstairs lights on for us in case we need anything and the outside pool bathroom will be open. Here, let's play. We have two hours to kill."

Jack dealt and Mira won the first three hands, once with an ace and a queen for Blackjack. Jack always tried to make twenty-one and took too many cards. He was always going over twenty-one. They played for about an hour when Jack gave up.

"How much longer Mira?"

"Mira checked her watch and told Jack they still had an hour. Jack laid down on his sleeping bag and propped his head up on his arm with a sigh. Mira pulled out her book and began to read.

"What are you reading?"

"Theodore Boone – Kid Lawyer. "

"Really, tell me about it."

"Well, it's about a thirteen year old boy whose parents are lawyers. He acts like a lawyer, helping out his friends or animals that have problems. I think you would like it. You have a lot in common. You and Theodore are both the only child of two lawyers. Do you want to be a lawyer some day?"

"I don't know what I want to be yet. I know my Dad works all the time and I am not sure I want to work that hard. Still he says he loves it. I know you want to be a scientist."

"I do, but I don't know what type of scientist. There're lots of different types. Well, either way, we have plenty of time to decide."

"Right. Will you read out loud? It will help pass the time."

So Mira began reading and sure enough the hour faded away. Jack peeked out of the tent door and Nugget rose up from the hole he dug for a bed. The light was out in Jack's parent's bedroom so he told Mira to get everything ready. She checked her clothes and the put on the backpack. The walkie talkie was clipped to her belt. Jack did the same and looked at Mira. She nodded and he turned out the lantern.

"Ten O'clock on the nose. Let's go."

Jack and Mira crept out of the darkened tent and quietly zipped the door closed. They walked over to the clear spot on the lawn to call up the tornado.

"Mariah" said Mira in her mind.

"Yes. Little One?"

"We want to go to Rome. Is there a nice quiet park near the center of the city?

"Yes. I know just the spot."

Jack and Mira held hands with Nugget between them. Mira nodded to Jack and Jack closed his eyes and knitted his brows in concentration. Mira covered a smile with her free hand. The wind began to swirl and Mira watched as Jack's yard disappeared

Stephen Meritt

Chapter 7

His Holiness Pope Francis rarely had a day of peace, a day when he could just sit and think about the troubles of the world and how his church might help. He had only been Pope for a short while and the problems both inside the church and outside were overwhelming. His assistant, Father Luigi, had informed him last night, as he was preparing for bed, that Friday there were no meetings scheduled. At last, he would be able to meditate in his favorite place – the Papal Garden. It is a beautiful garden with flowering bushes and quiet paths and benches. He could let his mind slowly work on the issues facing him. He liked to get up early. He had been rising with the sun his whole life and today would be no different.

He was walking down the special stairs that led from his apartment to the garden. He was thinking about how much he missed his home and the peace and quiet of the Argentina of his childhood. All old men must think this way at times - if only he could recapture just a tiny bit of his youth.

He never expected to be elected Pope. It's a tremendous privilege and a fearsome responsibility. It also took all real privacy from him. He couldn't travel or visit places without a whole entourage. He had large groups of advisors, servants, assistants, and security staff following him everywhere including news people taking pictures. He had to meet important people and make speeches anytime he went outside the Vatican City walls. The price of his election was fame and the loss of his freedom. All of this was whirling around in his mind as he stepped through the arches of the doorway to the garden.

He gave a big sigh. He walked slowly over to sit on his favorite bench nestled in the Azalea bushes. There was a view of a beautifully manicured small grassy lawn. It almost looked like a putting green the grass was so even. Elm trees provided shade around the lawn with flowers between the trees. It was so peaceful he could fall asleep. He heard birds chirping as he made himself comfortable with a book on his lap and put on his glasses one ear loop at a time. He was just about to close his eyes when he felt a breeze on his face and then the breeze became stronger. There was a slight roaring noise that became louder and louder and he saw a whirling tornado like funnel that stopped right in the middle of the lawn.

The roaring sound stopped and the funnel disappeared. To his great surprise, two children and a huge dog were standing in the middle of his lawn right where the tornado had been. They looked at him and he at them with open mouths. The children were wearing jeans. The boy had on a plaid shirt and the girl, a solid light blue shirt. The dog was a monster of a dog, but wearing a blue and gold bandana with an initial on it. He had on a blue collar with a metal tag which must be his dog license.

Mira saw the man first and Jack a second later. He had been looking at Nugget. Nugget was on alert and standing close to them, looking at the man who was sitting on a park bench. The man was not threatening in any way. He had a slight build and the slightly slumped shoulders of an older man. He wore glasses and had snow white hair that Mariah had whipped up around his small round white hat. He was wearing a white robe that came down to his ankles, white shoes and a large silver cross on a silver chain hung around his neck.

He put his hand up as if to wave a greeting with a nice smile.

"Mariah, I thought the park would be empty." Said Mira silently.

"It was, until just before I put you down. He is a holy man and will do you no harm."

After what seemed like a few minutes, but was more like a few seconds, the young girl stepped forward and addressed the man in English.

"I'm sorry that we disturbed you. We didn't think anyone would be in the park at this time of day. I'm Mira and this is Jack and our dog Nugget."

"Well, you are quite a surprise. My name is Francis. Welcome to my garden."

Before they could reply, Nugget gave a very low growl as four men came running around the path. Two of them were wearing suits and ties, but two were in a really wild costume. It had broad stripes of blue, red and orange that ran from head to toe. They had a funny metal helmet and one was carrying what looked like some kind of spear. Nugget immediately moved in front of Jack and Mira. His fur was puffed up and his tail straight out. He was obviously in protective mode.

The man in the white robe raised his hand and the four men immediately came to a halt staring at Nugget and the kids. One said something to the man in the white robe in what was most likely Italian. Neither Jack nor Mira understood what was being said. After a minute of conversation between the men and the man in the robe, they turned around and slowly left the park. Nugget relaxed and opened his mouth in a doggie smile as his sat down on his hind legs.

"I must apologize to you if my bodyguards frightened you. You see, the entire garden is covered with sensors that can detect movement. There are also cameras in various locations to alert the guards of any intruders. I think when you suddenly showed up on the sensors it set off a panic in the Swiss Guards office."

Jack cleared his throat and said "Swiss Guard?" Aren't we in Rome?"

The man smiled and said "Indeed you are young man. You are in the middle of Rome in the Papal Garden which is part of Vatican City. I take it from your stares that you are not Catholic, which means you don't know exactly where you are and who I am. Is that right?"

Both Mira and Jack just nodded their heads.

"But, you look kind of like a Rabbi" Said Mira.

The man looked startled for a moment and then began laughing. It was a real hardy, belly laugh. After a minute, he pulled a handkerchief out of his robe pocket and removed his glasses to wipe his eyes. When he was done, he put his glasses back on and took a deep breath.

"That was wonderful, thank you for brightening my day. It's amazing how a little humor can lift the spirit. I take it from your comment that you're Jewish. Am I correct?"

"Um, no sir. My Mom is Jewish and my Dad is Greek Orthodox. When I asked what I was they told me that when I was old enough to understand religion then I could choose what I would like to be. I thought you might be a Rabbi because when I went to my cousin's Bar Mitzvah the Rabbi had on a white robe and a small cap like yours that they called a Kippa."

The man reached up and touched his skull cap to make sure it was still there and smiled.

"How about you, Jack?"

"Well, my Mom is Methodist and my Dad is Catholic, but I want to be Jewish like Mira. She gets to celebrate Hanukkah and Christmas."

The man laughed again and said, "I sorry I am not laughing at you. It's just that it has been a long time since I've had a religious conversation with children, especially children who are not Catholic."

"Don't you have any children?" asked Jack.

"No. When I became a priest I agreed not to get married so I could devote all my time to helping others. Mira, you are somewhat right. You see a Rabbi is a teacher; it's a Jewish term for a man who has studied hard and made it his life's work to help others. I am a teacher too, but since I am Catholic and not Jewish, I am called a Priest."

"So that being said, let me give you a very brief little history lesson. Two thousand years ago St. Peter started the Catholic Church when he passed on the teachings of a Rabbi named Jesus Christ. At first the Romans fought against the new Christian religion, but eventually they all became Christians. As time passed, the leaders of Rome gave part of the city to the Church for its headquarters. That became Vatican City. It's a separate country within the City of Rome. The leaders of the Church always live and work in Vatican City. The head of the Church is called The Pope. He is like your President, only he is elected for life. I became the 266th Pope last year. I am called Pope Francis. Welcome to Vatican City and Rome. Now, if you would, please tell me how you came to be here."

"Could you give us a moment, Sir?"

Jack and Mira looked at each other and decided that they had to tell Pope Francis all about the traveling tornado.

"I'll tell him the story, Jack. Is that okay?"

Jack took a breath and nodded okay to Mira. They stepped a little closer and were facing Pope Francis when Mira began their story. She explained what had happened to Jack one day in the park near his home in West Hills, which is in the Los Angeles valley. She told the Pope all about Jack's experience in the Civil War and about their trips to Florida, Norway, Arizona and now Rome. She explained that they wanted to explore the world and how they found Nugget, or rather him finding them. They had come to Rome to see the Coliseum. She didn't mention Mariah.

"If I may ask, how did you happen to pick Rome?"

Mira explained about her Mom's teenage story about coming here with her Latin Club. She enjoyed seeing the Coliseum and eating in a small sidewalk café across the street.

"Well, that is quite a story and if I hadn't seen it with my own eyes I wouldn't have believed it was possible. This will require a lot of thought. So you are here as tourists. Would you like to see the Sistine Chapel and the Cathedral of St. Peter as well as the Coliseum? The Cathedral was named for St. Peter, our first Pope."

Jack and Mira looked at each other and nodded.

"We would love to, sir. Is Nugget going to be a problem?"

"No, no problem at all, but now that you've mentioned Nugget. I can see he is not an ordinary dog. He is quite regal. You don't know this, but I chose the name Francis after St. Francis of Assisi, the patron saint of animals. I also grew up in Argentina. Now you look surprised. As an Argentinian and an animal lover, I am familiar with the Mexican Gray Wolf. Is Nugget a Lobo by any chance?"

Jack nodded and said, "Yes Sir. He's also part dog according to our vet. Would you like to meet him?"

"I would indeed."

Nugget knew he was being talked about and smiled his doggie smile while giving his tail a small wag. At a signal from Jack he moved slowly forward until his nose was almost in Pope Francis' lap. He sniffed the Pope's hand and allowed the Pope to rub his head. The Pope broke into a huge smile and looked at Jack and Mira.

"Thank you very much for that privilege. Now, how about a tour? The Chapel and the Cathedral aren't open to the public until nine o'clock and it is only a little after 7:00 so we have time. Let me give you a personal tour. I rarely get to see it myself without lots of other people about."

Mira, Jack and Nugget followed Pope Francis over to a low building entrance with stone arches. Just as they entered a man in a black priest's suit opened the door.

"Good Morning, Father Luigi, I would like you to meet three new friends from America. Mira, Jack, Nugget, this is Father Luigi, he is my assistant."

"Pleased to meet you sir." Said Mira. Jack nodded.

Father Luigi gave Pope Francis an odd look and Pope Francis told him he would explain it all later. He asked Father Luigi to notify the Guard office that he would be taking the children on a tour of the Chapel and the Cathedral personally. The guards needed to unlock the private entrances and turn on the lights. He talked to Father Luigi for a minute in Italian and Father Luigi nodded and hurried away.

"Sometimes, it's nice to be in charge, but most of the time it's a real burden. Follow me."

Pope Francis led them through a maze of hallways and finally to a small door. He stopped before the door and told them that within was a special Chapel built ages ago as a place for Popes to pray. It was dull and drab so one Pope decided to have it painted with scenes from the Bible. He hired the famous painter named Michelangelo.

He opened the door and they stepped into a world of awe. It was impossible to take it all in. Mira and Jack just stood and looked at the walls and the magnificent ceiling. Everywhere they looked they saw the most beautiful paintings. They all walked quietly through the Chapel, everyone looking at the various paintings, even the Pope. He began to point out particular scenes and talked about the stories.

After about an hour of admiring the paintings, the Pope told them he was going to take them to the Cathedral now.

Mira turned to him and thanked him. She had never imagined such a beautiful building. Jack nodded that he felt the same.

Mira asked, "Why don't you come here all the time?"

"Well," smiled the Pope. "I would like to spend more time in here, but we allow all the public to tour the Chapel and if I were here it would cause a big mess. Everyone would want to talk to me or ask for something. I am not allowed to go into crowds, I have to have guards with me all the time, just like your President."

"That's sad." Said Jack.

"That's why I am enjoying visiting here with you. It's a joy to see it again and to watch you as you see it for the first time. I hope you will come back to see it again someday."

"We will." Said Jack and Mira in unison.

Pope Francis then led them through another small door and up some stairs to another small door. He opened it up and smiled as the kids saw the biggest building they had ever entered. They had come in through a small doorway in the back of the Cathedral. It was silent and massive. Mira felt tiny as she looked around. The Pope enjoyed telling them all about the Cathedral as they walked around. It is the biggest Catholic Church in the whole world. It even had marks on the floor where other churches would fit if placed inside St. Peter's Cathedral. It was totally mind blowing. Mira and Jack had seen many buildings in LA and other cities that they thought were big, but this just out shined everything.

"This is all your church? Asked Jack.

Pope Francis laughed and said. "Not mine like I own it. I am its appointed caretaker. I didn't always live here. I came from Argentina when I was elected to be the Pope. To tell you the truth I really miss Argentina."

"So why did you come if it so much trouble and you can't walk around to enjoy it all?"

"That's a very good question, Jack. I guess you could call it my duty. My job is to look after it to the best of my ability for the sake of others, even if it means giving up something I love."

"I guess I understand."

"You will one day, Jack. Now I have a surprise for you."

He pressed a button on a small device from his robe pocket and Father Luigi appeared as if magic.

"Yes, Your Holiness?"

"Is everything prepared Luigi?"

"Yes, sir"

Pope Francis turned to Jack, Mira and Nugget and told them that he had Father Luigi arrange a car to take them to the Coliseum. They would have their own personal guide. After their tour, they would be taken to the café across from the Coliseum for a snack before coming back to meet him again in his garden.

Jack and Mira were stunned. This was more than they could have even imagined. They smiled and thanked the Pope.

"No need to thank me. You have given an old man something very special today. While you're on tour, I have some deep thinking to do. I will talk to you in the garden when you come back. I may have a favor to ask. Now go and enjoy."

Chapter 8

Mira looked back and waved to Pope Francis as they followed Father Luigi out another small door. He explained that the big doors would be open at nine o'clock to allow the public to visit and all the small doors that led into the Vatican would be locked. They wound their way through several buildings including a massive library that caused Mira to pause. Father Luigi stopped and smiled at Mira.

"This is my favorite place", he said.

"It is one of the biggest libraries in the world with the largest numbers of ancient books. One room has nothing, but scrolls."

Mira replied, "Maybe one day I could read some of the books here."

"I am sure that could be possible someday, but you might need to learn some other languages first. Plus you must also be a scientist or researcher."

"Okay"

They proceeded through part of the library and into another building with a door to a driveway. A black car was waiting for them with a driver. Another man in a priest's suit was holding open the back door. Father Luigi introduced them to Father James who was from New York.

"He had been studying the ancient Roman Empire in the library here and will be your guide to the Coliseum today."

Father James smiled at them and gestured for them to get in the car. Nugget hopped right in and Jack and Mira followed. Mira waved to Father Luigi as they left for their tour of the Coliseum. Father James climbed in the front seat next to the driver. He turned around to explain that, at the request of the Pope, the authorities would allow them to enter through a special portal that led to where the gladiators were housed. The public was normally not allowed in that section of the ruins.

They arrived at the Coliseum after a short but exciting ride. There were lots of horns honking and the driver kept mumbling things under his breath at the other drivers. Father James smiled since he spoke Italian and understood what the driver was saying. Mira always thought the traffic was bad in LA, but Rome was pure chaos. People and cars seemed to going in every direction all at the same time.

When they first saw the Coliseum, it made up for the ride. Right there in the middle of this modern city was the huge ancient Roman building. Parts of it had collapsed and other parts appeared to be under repair. Father James began to explain the problems that the traffic and the modern day atmosphere had

had on the old stone structure. He said there was a project underway to help preserve the Coliseum for future generations, but it required a lot of money.

They drove up to a gate and the guard waved them right though to a covered area where they were able to park. Mira noticed that some people were watching them. She asked Father James about that and he told them that the people were curious because the car had the special license tags of the Vatican. They were wondering if someone special was in the car and who it might be. They climbed out of the car and a few people took pictures as they moved into the building.

"Jack said, "They act like we are stars."

Father James said, "Just ignore them, when they realize you aren't someone famous they will delete their photos."

They walked into the building and were immediately covered by a dark shadowy hall with a long high arch. Father James began to tell them about the entrance where the gladiators were brought when they first arrived in Rome. They saw the cells where the slaves and gladiators lived and the areas where they practiced to fight in the arena. It was fascinating and Jack was in heaven. Nugget sniffed at every nook and cranny. They soon arrived at the base of the arena and Father explained how it was a stage-like floor where doors could be opened and closed to allow animals to enter from their pens.

He told them about great chariot races and even staged sea battles when the arena was filled with water. They spent two hours wandering about with Father James. He knew everything about the Coliseum. At times, they were in mobs of tourists, who were careful not to get too close because of Nugget. He was on a leash, but no one had ever seen a dog like Nugget. Father James told them there was one other area which they would tour.

They walked around the raised hallways and came to an area that was blocked off with a velvet rope. There is a sign that said NO ENTRE. Father James unhooked the rope and let them through then rehung the rope to keep others out. They walked through a large arch way that was carved with all sorts of battle scenes and profiles of different Romans. They went down a few steps and found themselves in an elevated box in the middle of the arena seats. They could see the whole Coliseum.

"This is the royal box where the Emperors of Rome and their guests watched the fights and decided the fate of the fallen gladiators."

Jack stepped up to the low wall and held out the right hand with his thumb sticking up. Father James smiled and said.

"Another gladiator lives to fight another day. Okay, let's go get a snack."

On the way out Mira stopped to go to the bathroom and Jack thanked Father James for a wonderful tour. He asked him how long he planned to stay in Rome and said he didn't know. He could be here his whole life or they may send him somewhere else to teach.

"It's kind of like being in the army. You go where they send you."

Mira returned and they went to the car. Father James told the driver something and he grinned.

They shot out of the parking area and back into traffic. They went around a circle so fast that Jack and Mira slid to one side of the car. Nugget had his head out a partially opened window with his tongue hanging out. He was having a great time. Soon they came to a stop on the side of the street across from the front side of the Coliseum. Mira looked out the window and there was a little sidewalk café. It had small tables on the sidewalk with red tablecloths and umbrellas. Waiters were serving customers food and wine.

Father James helped them out of the car and the driver joined them for an early lunch. The driver kept smiling and Mira's curiosity got the better of her so she asked Father James why the driver was so happy. Father James smiled and said.

"Well, he is getting a free lunch and he loves parking in a no parking zone. The traffic police can't give him a ticket because we have diplomatic plates on the car which allows us to park anywhere we want. It's a perk of the Vatican being a separate country. We try not to abuse the privilege, but sometimes it's fun as well as convenient."

Both Mira and Jack had spaghetti and the waiter brought a pork chop out for Nugget on his own plate. Father James and the driver both had a fish plate and a glass of wine. After they were done, Mira offered to pay for their lunch, but Father James refused telling them that they were the guests of the Pontiff. They hopped back in the car for the trip back to the Papal Garden. The ride was short and fun with the driver enjoying himself tooting the horn often. It was noon when they arrived back at the Vatican and Father James said goodbye as he handed them off to Father Luigi.

Mira thanked Father James again and asked if he was coming with them into the Garden. Father James smiled and shook his head.

"Only very special people get to talk to the Pope. There are thousands of us working and studying here in the Vatican and if we all stopped to talk to His Holiness then he would never get anything done. Someday, if I am fortunate, I may get to meet him. Bye now."

"Bye." Jack and Mira said together. Nugget wagged his tail.

Father Luigi walked them into the garden and up to the Pope who was still sitting on the bench where they had first met him. He smiled and asked if they had a good tour.

"Great!" said Jack.

"It was wonderful and Father James knew so much about the Coliseum. He did a great job of showing us around and taking us to lunch. Thank you very much."

Pope Francis smiled and nodded to Father Luigi who nodded in return. Jack asked if he could be excused for a few minutes and Father Luigi told Jack to follow him. As they walked off and Nugget was checking out the bushes, Pope Francis looked at Mira and patted the bench next to him. Mira sat down next to the Pope and waited as he cleared his throat.

"Mira, I have been contemplating everything that you told me about your traveling here and I know it's true, but I think I haven't heard the whole story. Do you know what contemplating means?

"Yes, sir. It means thinking about something."

"Excellent! After much thought, I came to the conclusion there is something you haven't told me yet nor Jack. Am I right?"

"Yes, sir." Mira took a deep breath and Pope Francis waited patiently to hear her story. Mira began at Jack's first adventure and explained how she started hearing giggling. She told him what had happened when they went to Paradise and about her conversations with Mariah. His eyes seem to get bigger each time she explained what was happening and that it was really Mariah controlling the tornado, not Jack. With a sigh he looked at Mira.

"It seems that you and Jack have been given a truly miraculous experience. To me, it's a confirmation of the Holy One to whom I have devoted my entire life. It's a privilege very few of mankind have gotten. Mariah is a direct creation of God to help make and protect the Earth. Can she hear you all the time? "

"If she wishes to. I don't really know. I just think about her or talk to her aloud and she answers.

I guess she could get tired of being with us and not respond."

"Never, I have committed myself to you and Jack for your lifetimes my dear."

Mira smiled and Pope Francis noticed it.

"Did she just speak to you?"

"Yes, Sir"

"Hmm, would you ask her something for me?" Mira nodded. "Ask her if I would be allowed to travel with you and Jack somewhere, please?"

"I heard him and agree to take the four of you anywhere you would like to go."

Mira said aloud. "Thank you. Mariah said yes, she will take us anywhere you want."

Pope Francis' face lit up like a kid in a candy store.

"Marvelous! Here comes Jack. Will you tell him of my request? I would like to visit Argentina. I miss it so much it clouds my thinking. I also have a sick friend that I would like to see."

Jack walked up and Nugget came back from somewhere in the garden.

"Jack, Pope Francis asked if we could take him traveling with us. He would like to go back for a visit to Argentina. Is that alright with you?"

"Awesome! Yes sir. I would love to go. Do you think we will see a gaucho?"

Pope Francis laughed and asked Jack how he knew about gauchos. Jack told him about his geography class where they studied South America. Gauchos were Argentinian cowboys. Pope Francis pushed the button again on the little device and Father Luigi appeared a minute later. Pope Francis spoke to him for a few minutes and then he left. Pope Francis nodded to Jack and Mira and they all walked to the lawn as a breeze began to swirl around. Pope Francis asked them to wait one moment as he took off his white robe and carefully folded it. He also took off his white cap. Now he looked like any other old person in a baggy pair of tan slacks and a white collarless shirt. He smiled at them as he hid the robe and cap under a bush.

They all held hands, Jack stood next to Mira and Nugget was between Mira and Pope Francis. Jack said.

"Where would you like to go?"

Pope Francis smiled and said, "I would like to visit an old favorite village of mine near the Andes Mountains called Calingasta."

Almost before he could finish his sentence, the wind began to swirl and they were off on another adventure. None of them saw Father Luigi watching from a nearby Azalea hedge. Father closed his eyes and crossed himself as he said a prayer for his Pope and the children.

Stephen Meritt

Chapter 9

They arrived in Argentina in the late afternoon. It should have been evening with the time change, but then Mariah could adjust time. They landed in a farm field just south of the village and Pope Francis led them to the main street. It was not much bigger than the street in the ghost town of Paradise, only the buildings were still standing. Some were painted and on others the paint was peeling off and they looked run down. They came to a village square where four streets or roads all met. They were not paved roads, but packed dirt. On the north side of the square the street continued on to some trees and disappeared. To the west framed by the mountains was a small church. Jack couldn't see anything to the east. It looked like rolling hills or a big field. Pope Francis saw him looking and said.

"That is the start of the western edge of the Great Pampas. Almost all of Argentina is a great flat area similar to your American Great Plains. We raise lots and lots of cattle which is why we have gauchos. We send food all over the world. On the other side of the Andes is Chile. "

They walked into the square and around to the left where there is a small café. The town was strangely quiet.

"Something is not right", said Pope Francis. "Oh, by the way, if we should meet anyone please don't refer to me as Pope Francis or Your Holiness. My first name is Jorge. It's Spanish for George and my middle name is Mario. When I was young my close friends all called me Mario. I would like you to do that too. Okay?"

"Yes, sir." They said together.

There was a lone man sitting at the café with his back to them as they walked around the square. He wore baggie jeans and a black shirt and had white hair and maybe a beard, but it was hard to see from where they were standing. Mario began to smile and said,

"There is my oldest friend, Wilfredo. We started out together as young priests. He is my confessor, which means that he is sworn never to say anything about what I tell him. I haven't seen him in a very long time. We have both become old men and I may never get the chance to see him again. That's why I asked to come here. You see, I found out he has been sick and can no longer travel. If I came here as Pope - well, you understand the problems I have traveling now."

Both Mira and Jack nodded. Jack noticed that Nugget was on the alert and busy running around lifting his legs almost everywhere. He thought it was just his curiosity of a new place. Everyone would find out differently soon. They continued walking around the square and still the Priest didn't notice them. At the last minute he turned around and stared as if he had seen a ghost. He jumped up knocking over his chair and almost upsetting his bottle of wine. He stammered and said something in rapid Spanish and reached out bowing over Mario's right hand, kissing a big gold ring that the Pope wore on his fourth finger.

"Willie, Willie, no need for formalities between us in this place. Please my old friend call me Mario, now sit down and tell me what is happening. Where are all the people? This was always such a loud and noisy village. Oh, May I introduce my friends and travel companions Senorita Mira and Senor Jack and somewhere around here is their dog, Nugget."

"Oh, Your Holiness, sorry Mario, this poor village has seen better days. The villagers are afraid to go out in the evenings anymore. We have been having a terrible time with a pack of wild dogs. Your friends should call their dog in before something happens. We can all go in the café when the pack arrives."

"Has the Government not done anything Willie?"

"Well, they are discussing having a new law to start hunting the dogs but nothing has reached us here. It seems to be a problem throughout Argentina. We are such a small village that there is no one to protect us. We have no hunters here. We stay indoors except in the middle of the day when the dogs rest. BY ALL THE SAINTS! What is that?"

Nugget had just reappeared and Willie saw him for the first time. Everyone laughed while the poor priest looked bewildered. Nugget came over and sat down next to Mira and Mario introduced Nugget to Wilfredo.

"He is a monster. I have never seen such a dog. What is he and where did he come from?"

Mario nodded to Mira and she explained what Nugget was. The priest's eyes seemed to get bigger for a while. Just as Mira finished explaining about Nugget, they heard a bunch of yapping and barking from the north end of town near the forest. Within minutes, a medium size brown dog appeared around the house nearest the north side of the square. It was sniffing the ground that Nugget had previously marked. It looked as if the dog was shivering and looking around. Other barks could be heard and soon there were four dogs near the house and some others moving in.

"We had best move inside now." Said Willie.

At that moment, Nugget lifted his head and let out a blood curdling howl. It was something none of them had ever heard before even in the mountains of Arizona. Mira and Jack were stunned as were the two priests. Nugget stood up and the dog pack all stared at Nugget. Then before anyone could react, Nugget took off with a mighty leap that must have been twenty feet. He ran right at the dog pack which turned as one and ran. They disappeared around the corner of the building with Nugget on their tails. Then they heard the most frightful sound of dogs fighting, yowling and crying. Suddenly, everything went silent. Everyone waited, listening carefully, but heard absolutely nothing. Jack started to get up, but Mira stopped him with her hand on his arm.

"Look"

Nugget came prancing around the corner with his head and tail high. His beautiful blue and gold bandana was in shreds. As he came closer they could all see blood on his muzzle and head. Mira gasped and Jack jumped up to run over to Nugget. Nugget greeted Jack in his usual manner. Mario joined them and asked to take a look at Nugget. He checked Nugget over thoroughly and smiled.

"Don't worry; the blood is not Nugget's. It seems as if Nugget is not hurt at all."

Mira let out a sob of relief and Jack just sat down in the dirt. Once they had gathered themselves together, they hugged and petted Nugget. They had just started walking back to the café, when a man dressed like a cowboy came running down the street toward the café. Jack's mouth fell open and he whispered – "A Gaucho."

Father Wilfred smiled at Jack and said, "Indeed, that is Senor Sanchez and he is a gaucho. The dog packs have been killing his cattle. He has tried to chase them off, but they keep coming back."

"Why didn't he shoot them?"

"Our gauchos are not like your American cowboys. Instead of guns they carry Bolas. Do you know what they are?

"I saw a picture once. It's three balls on a rope."

"That's close. It's three ropes tied at one end, each with a weighted ball on the other end. You swing them over your head, faster and faster and then throw it at your target. If you don't miss, the balls and ropes wrap around the target and get all tangled together, capturing the target. Senor Sanchez tried it on the dogs, but if he stopped one dog the others protect it until it can chew through the ropes."

By now the gaucho, had reached them and still panting said,

"Father that big dog killed all the pack dogs. There is not a single one left. We are free. The village must celebrate this miracle."

"I agree. If it's okay with your friends? Mario?"

"It's an excellent idea, Willie. Why not have someone ring the church bell to summon the villagers."

Willie turned to the gaucho and told him to spread the word and send his son to ring the bell.

"Please tell everyone you see to bring some food and drink."

The Pope looked over at Mira and Jack and smiled.

"You best get some water and clean up our hero while Willie and I have a little chat. We'll be back shortly"

"Yes sir."

(continued)

Jack went into the café and asked for agua and pointed at the cloth napkins because he didn't remember their Spanish name. The café owner nodded and gave Jack a pot of water and some napkins which he carried outside to the porch. He and Mira washed Nugget's head and shoulders and dried him with the napkins. Mira returned the pot and the napkins and told the café owner, gracias.

A few minutes later Mario and Willie returned and Willie had a funny expression on his face as he looked at the three of them. Mira immediately figured out the Pope had told his friend about them. She knew from Mario's explanation of a confession that Willie would never say anything. There were now people coming from all parts of the village carrying baskets toward the church. From the way Nugget was licking his lips, they were carrying food. They all sat for a few minutes to let the people gather.

The Pope and Willie rose together and Mario told Jack that it would be best to put the leash on Nugget even if he didn't really need one. Otherwise the villagers might get nervous. Jack leashed Nugget and they all began walking to the church. Everyone else had already gone inside, so they came last. When they entered there was complete silence. Willie stopped to put on a black robe and he and Mario both touched a stone bowl of water and crossed themselves.

Willie, in his Priest robe, walked up the center aisle of the church first. Mario and Mira followed and Jack came last holding Nugget on the leash. Father Willie and Mario both bowed to the large cross behind the Bible stand and crossed themselves again. Mario pointed to a pew in the front of the church that had been left open and Mira sat down with Mario next to her. The Priest gestured for Jack to bring Nugget up front with him next to the stand with the big Bible on it.

Jack stood there with Nugget facing the villagers while the Priest crossed himself again and began speaking in Spanish. It sounded to Mira as if he was saying some prayers and the congregation all said something in Spanish and crossed themselves. Then when everyone was silent the Priest gave a long speech. In the speech, Mira heard their names, Mira, Jack and Nugget. Mario leaned over and whispered to Mira that Willie was telling the story of Nugget's brave defense of their village. There was apparently a lot said about Nugget and the Priest pointed to him several times. There were oohs and aahs from the people. Then he said in English.

"Today is forever more to be known in our Village as the Fiesta del Perro".

Everybody stood and applauded Nugget. Mira and Jack smiled because they knew enough Spanish to know he said Festival of the Dog. After the applause died down, the people began setting up tables with all types of food. There were a lot of beef dishes which Nugget approved of in typical doggie fashion. He let everyone pet him and was especially gentle with the little children who grabbed his fur. He was rewarded with lot of handouts which really set his tail wagging.

The party began to thin out after a while and people were cleaning up. Mira and Jack helped and Nugget licked the floor. Mario and Willie paused from their conversations and came over to them.

"Well, I think it's time we headed back."

Willie and Mario hugged each other and Willie hugged Mira, Jack and Nugget. He barely even had to bend over to hug Nugget. All the remaining people said "adios". Jack, Mira, and Nugget walked behind Father Willie and the Pope back to the square where they first met Father Willie. Father Willie turned to Jack and Mira and told them to come back to visit when they could. Mr. Sanchez and his Gauchos would be happy to take them out to round up cattle. This made Jack very happy. They left Father Willie at the café and turned right on the street leading to the field where Mariah had brought them. It was dusk when they reached the field and held hands again as the tornado once again lifted them into the sky.

Chapter 10

In what seemed like just a few minutes, they arrived back on the lawn in the Papal Garden. Mira said a silent thank you to Mariah.

"You're welcome little one."

Mario went back to the bush where he had hidden his robe and Kippa. In a few seconds he had returned to being Pope Francis. He smiled at Jack and Mira and watched Nugget sniffing around. He went back to his favorite bench and beckoned Jack and Mira to join him.

"That was perhaps the most incredible and wondrous thing that has ever happened to me. You children have renewed my faith. I don't think I could ever repay you. Please thank Mariah for me."

"I already did."

"Tell him he's welcome."

She said, "You're welcome."

"Tell who what? Said Jack.

"I'll explain later, Jack."

Jack nodded and Mira thought a moment and said.

"We don't need any pay. We just came to visit the Coliseum and you gave us so much more, when you could have thrown us out. We never meant to intrude in your garden."

Jack agreed and Nugget returned and placed his head in the Pope's lap just as if he understood every word.

"You really have a most remarkable dog, but then you knew that didn't you. Before you go,

I would like to give you something." He pressed the button on the little call unit and Father Luigi appeared carrying a box in his hands which he gave to the Pope. Some distance behind Father Luigi stood Father James. Mira and Jack smiled and gave him a wave which he returned.

Pope Francis smiled and said, "I decided that Father Luigi was overworked, so I arranged for him to have an assistant. I hope you approve."

They both nodded enthusiastically.

Pope Francis then reached in the box and brought out gold coins, each in a clear plastic pouch with a snap. They were the size of a quarter. He gave each of them a gold coin. Mira looked at it and it had a profile of the Pope on one side and the front of St. Peter's Cathedral on the other. There were funny sounding words around the Pope's face. Mira tried to pronounce them, but wasn't sure she did it right. The Pope smiled and said it was Latin. On the other side there was more Latin above the Cathedral and English below it. The English said "Trusted Friend".

"These are very special coins which you should keep safe. It will allow you immediate permission to visit me anytime. You just show it to anyone and they will bring you right to me or any future Pope when I am gone. I will see to it that the story of your deeds and these coins are passed down from Pope to Pope so that someday even your children or grandchildren can use them. If, in your travels, you're ever in need of help of any kind just show the coin to any priest and they will do everything in their power to help."

Then he reached into the box again and brought out a third coin. It was identical to theirs, but had a hole on the top with a clip.

"This is a special coin to hang on Nugget's collar. When he has it on no one can keep him out. He will be able to accompany you as well. He saved the village and my friend Willie and I will always be in your debt."

Mira and Jack were stunned. They didn't know what to think. This was so beyond anything they expected. Finally, Mira said a very quiet "thank you" as did Jack. They carefully put the coins in the zipper pockets of their backpacks. Jack kept Nugget's coin.

Pope Francis looked thoughtful for a minute and said,

"If I may, I would like to make a suggestion for a trip. Think about visiting with the Dalai Lama. He is the head of the Buddhist Religion and was from Tibet near Mount Everest. He is a friend of mine and I am sure he would love to meet you. I understand he will be visiting a monastery in the State of Utah shortly.

"That sounds interesting. Thank you." Said Jack.

Mira looked at her watch and saw that it was five o'clock in the morning in LA.

"We need to go, Jack."

They all stood up and Pope Francis gave them each a big hug, saying "I will think of you each night when I say prayers." He petted Nugget and said goodbye as the three of them walked over to the lawn.

The breeze started and as the Pope and his two assistants withdrew as the breeze became a tornado. Jack, Mira and Nugget disappeared leaving Pope Francis smiling and the Fathers Luigi and James standing with their mouths open. Pope Francis turned to them and said.

"This is a miracle that you will never be able to talk about except between us and your future Pontiffs. You do understand don't you?"

"Yes, Your Holiness."

Chapter 11

Mira, Jack and Nugget arrived in Jack's back yard at 5:30 in the morning. They had been up all night on their grand adventure. They looked at each other and were silent. Finally, Mira unzipped the tent door, took off her backpack and got in her sleeping bag. Jack followed and Nugget circled around and around in the hole he had dug before they left.

An hour later, Jack's Father came out to the tent dressed in his suit to go to work. Nugget looked up at him and wagged his tail. Mr. Jones gave him a rub and Nugget put his head back down on his paws. Mr. Jones carefully unzipped the door a little bit so he could peek in. There were Jack and Mira sound asleep in their sleeping bags. He closed the tent and said to Nugget.

"I bet you were playing all night. They'll probably sleep all day. Watch over them. Good dog."

Mr. Jones went back through the house and left a note on the kitchen counter for Mrs. Jones, who was still sleeping. He told her the kids were fine and sleeping like babies. He would see her later at dinner.

Mrs. Jones was up by eight 'clock and had her coffee and some breakfast. The phone rang about nine o'clock and it was Mira's Mom.

"Are they bothering you?"

"Are you kidding? They're still asleep. Mike checked on them before he left and his note said they were sleeping like babies. They must have been up half the night. I'm about to have a second coffee. Do you want to come over for coffee with muffins or bagel?"

"Sure, give me ten minutes. We can catch up on our gossip. It's been awhile since we have had time alone. I'm taking Mira to practice her skating after lunch."

"Perfect. I am taking Jack shopping. He'll make a big fuss about it, but he has outgrown almost everything he owns."

Helen and Gray spent the morning talking about school since Gray was President of the PTA. Helen helps out when Gray is off on a job. Helen used to work, but retired when Jack was born. She said she has been thinking about doing some part time work now that Jack was in school and didn't require as much supervision. She would just have to arrange things around his after school activities. It is hard to do part time law because law problems take up a lot of time and it's hard to say to someone, sorry I've got to go to my son's soccer practice.

At 11:30 Helen said "it's time to get the kids up, shall we?"

They walked out the patio door and around to the side yard. Nugget jumped up and ran to greet them. He was all doggie smiles and wagging his tail. He didn't need as much sleep and was happy to have someone to play with. He was getting bored waiting for Jack and Mira. Helen and Gray both gave him a rub and Helen said she would feed him as soon as they woke the kids.

"Here Nugget, you can help."

Helen unzipped the tent door and pointed in to Nugget. Nugget yipped and ran right in the tent. He walked all over Jack and Mira, licking their faces. He put his head and front paws on the ground while he had his hind legs straight up like he was going to pounce on them. He wanted to play. Mira giggled and laughed as she got up. Jack on the other hand didn't want to get up and tried to hide in his sleeping bag. Nugget grabbed the end of the bag nearest the door and began pulling Jack and his sleeping bag out of the tent. Their Moms were laughing.

"Time to get up sleepy heads. You missed breakfast, but you can wash up and have lunch. Mira you are going skating after lunch and Jack, we are going clothes shopping."

"AAH MOM! Do I have to?"

"Yes, now the both of you go wash up while we make you some lunch. After lunch you can pick up the cards that are now spread all over the yard and put away the tent."

"Yes, Mam." They both said.

Jack ran upstairs to his room to wash up, while Mira went to the downstairs guest bath. She remembered to take her backpack with her which had a change of clothes. She undressed and washed her face and hands. She brushed her teeth with her finger and then put on her fresh clothes from the backpack. She redid her pony tail and put her dirty clothes in the backpack. She bumped the coin in the zipper as she was closing the backpack which made her smile. When she was ready she went into the kitchen. She was chatting with her Mom while Mrs. Jones made grilled cheese sandwiches.

Jack returned and his Mom took one look and sent him back upstairs to change his clothes. He had washed up, but didn't bother to change clothes. He was not happy, but he was hungry. It didn't take him long to change. While they were eating, Mrs. Jones filled Nugget's bowl. After lunch they all went outside and began cleaning up. Mira's Mom showed them the game 52 pickup. They were not amused, but understood the joke. It didn't take long to fold the tent and store it in its pouch. They shook out the sleeping bags and rolled them up to be ready to use another time. Jack took the lantern back to the garage. When everything was done, Mira gave Jack and Nugget big hugs and she and her Mom walked back to her house.

"I had a great time Mom. Thanks."

"You're welcome, Kiddo. You and Jack must have been up you very late to have slept all morning."

"We talked and played cards. I beat Jack at Black Jack. When he got really bored, I read my book to him. He really liked the story of Theodore Boone. We finished the whole book, 263 pages. After a while we just fell asleep. Did you and Dad have fun?"

"We did indeed. We went to the Daily Grill for dinner and then a late movie called "Wild" with Reese Witherspoon. It's about a lady who hiked a thousand miles of our coast line. We didn't get home until late and went right to bed. Now go say Hi to your Dad and change into your skating clothes."

Mira ran into the house and into the office to say Hi to her Dad. He gave her a kiss and asked if she had a good time.

"We had a great time, thanks Dad."

"No problem, Pumpkin. I love you."

Stephen Meritt

Chapter 12

A week had gone by since Jack and Mira had traveled to Rome and Argentina. She was watching the news with her parents one evening after dinner when a reporter said that Pope Francis announced that he would be planning to visit the Americas next year. He hoped to stop in Boston, Washington, Houston, and Los Angeles before going Mexico, Brazil and Argentina. He is expected to draw huge crowds and security will be tight. President Obama said he will be discussing the mid-east peace process and other sensitive issues with the Pope and a State Dinner will be held in his honor.

The reporter went on to say that insiders noted that the Pope seemed to have a renewed vigor and was being very active. They showed a picture of the Pope waving from his balcony to the crowds in St. Peter's Square in front of the Cathedral. There were two priests in black suits with high white collars behind him. Mira smiled.

"Mom, will we get to see the Pope when he comes to LA?"

"I don't know. It's very hard to get to see him up close, because he is so famous. We might be able to get tickets to his speech if someone I know is managing the event."

"Why don't you manage it? You're a stage manager."

"Well, you never know, but they usually have their own people handle all that. It would be a miracle if they called me."

Mira smiled.

Jack and Mira were having really good days in school as it was drawing to a close. June was fast approaching and school would be out for the summer. She was looking forward to spending the Fourth of July with her Grandparents in Florida. They would also visit her other Grandmother in Maryland. Jack was going to a day camp for a month and said he was going to learn how to ride a horse. He thought they might need another gaucho in Calingasta now that the dogs are gone. Mira told him that she would see him when she got back from Florida and Maryland and they could begin planning a new trip.

"Mount Everest sounded very interesting."

"It's beautiful. I like to nap on it. In the summer people are always trying to climb it. Sometimes, if they disturb me, I blow them off. I would be glad to take you there."

"You looked lost for a second, Mira. Is anything wrong?"

"No, just thinking. I'll see you tomorrow."

School ended with a nice class party with cupcakes and ice cream being served. All the kids had summer plans. Some were taking long trips out of the country; others were going on trips in the country, like Mira. A few were going to sleep away camps and the rest to day camps like Jack and

Mira after her visit to her Grandparents. Mira was very happy as she packed up all her desk stuff and cleaned out her cubby. She waited in the play yard with the other kids for her Mom or Dad to pick her up. It wasn't long before she spotted her Mom's car parking in the lot. She gathered up her stuff and met her Mom half way.

"Hi, Kiddo. How did the party go?"

"Great Mom. I'm going to miss school."

"Well, I think you can find something to occupy your mind for the summer. You know, good books, a visit to the east coast, day camp. Jack will be around most of it so who knows what you will find."

They arrived at their car and after her Mom unlocked it, she climbed into the back seat and put on her seat belt. It was then that she noticed a funny newspaper on the seat. Her Mom never buys newspapers and when she does it's a really big one. She liked the New York Times because she used to work in the theatres in New York before she got married and moved to LA. This newspaper was smaller, like a big magazine. The title was in big red letter and said The National Inquirer.

Then she saw it and her eyes got big. Right below the magazine's name was a headline that said "Huge Wolf Stalking Kids in Roman Coliseum" and under was a rather fuzzy picture of two kids in the coliseum with a huge dog with a blurry wrap around his neck standing behind them. She never thought of people with cell phones taking pictures of them. She didn't have a cell phone so she didn't think about pictures.

"What's the matter, Kiddo? Cat got you tongue?"

"Umm, Mom?"

"I got that magazine while waiting in line at Ralph's. That means the whole country will see it. What, still nothing to say, Kiddo? Why don't read the article on the way home."

Silently, Mira began to read the article while her Mom drove. Her mind was racing in all directions. Does anyone else suspect? What about all her friends and their parents who were at her birthday party? They've all seen Nugget. Would they make the connection? Do Jack's parents read this magazine?

"Various people, who were touring the famous Roman Coliseum a few weeks ago, were stunned to catch glimpses of a tremendous wolf like creature that seemed to be stalking children through the narrow winding passages of the Coliseum ruins. This is the only photograph we were able to find thanks to a quick thinking visitor who happened to be taking pictures of her family when the creature passed nearby. Roman authorities were notified and said they would investigate. There has been no other reported sighting of the creature. Zoo officials report no missing animals, but admit that the picture, although very blurry, seems to resemble a canis lupus. Anyone having any information on this incident is asked to contact the National Inquirer."

Oh man, what do I do now? Mom obviously knows. Others might not recognize Nugget from the fuzzy picture, but anyone close to us will. I must warn Jack in case someone says something. He needs to be prepared.

As if reading her mind, her Mom's cell phone rang. She has Bluetooth in the car which identified the caller as Dad. In this case, it didn't mean Mira's Dad, but her Mom's. Her Mom accepted the call.

"Hi Dad. What's going on?

"Hi Gray. Are you in the car?

"Yep, and Mira is here too. We are on the way home from school. Today was her last day."

"Hi Sweetie. How are you? We can't wait for you to visit us in just a few more weeks. I am planning to take you fishing again. Grandma Sandi has already starting baking petit fours.

"I can't wait either."

"By the way, Gray, have you by any chance seen the National Inquirer?"

"Well as a matter of fact, we just got one today in the grocery store. Mira was reading the article when you called."

"Well, I just wanted to call to tell you guys not to worry. I am pretty sure no one will think that's Nugget."

"Thanks Dad. We'll call you after dinner."

"Great. Love you both. Kisses."

"Love you too, Kisses. Bye."

Mom hit the disconnect button on her steering wheel and didn't say anything for a minute.

"You understand that we are going to have to talk when we get home. Don't you?"

"Yes Mam."

A few minutes later they pulled in the driveway. Mira had a little trouble unlatching her seat belt, but finally managed it.

"Say Hi to your Dad and put your school stuff away. When you finish, wash up and we'll have dinner. We can talk after your Father has a chance to read the article."

Mira walked slowly in the front door and took off her shoes. Her Dad was in the office as usual.

"Hi Dad. I'm home and school is out for the summer."

"Really, already. I thought you had at least six more weeks. Now I am going to be forced to entertain you day and night Pumpkin Head. I'll never get any work done. Maybe I should let you program this diagram. You know, to earn your keep."

"Dad!"

"Welcome, home. Let me finish this segment and we'll play guitar until dinner is ready. Okay Pumpkin?"

"Sure Dad."

Mira felt better and ran into her room with the school backpack. She set it down on her desk and began pulling out the papers, pencils and books. She put the books on her book shelf and the pencils in the pencil holder on her desk. She went through the papers and threw most of them in the trash can. She shook out her backpack and then hung it on a hook inside her closet next to her camping backpack which was still full and ready to go again.

With a sigh, Mira walked over to her bed post and picked up her walkie talkie. She looked at it for a minute, unsure if she should call Jack now or later. Later, she put the walkie talkie back on the post. I'll talk to him after I talk to my parents. She looked at her backpack again and went to the zipper pocket. There was the coin, all shiny in its plastic pouch. Now is when she could use a little help, but Pope Francis was a long way away. After a deep breath, she returned the coin to the pocket and went to the bathroom to wash up. She could hear her Dad tuning a guitar.

She met her Dad in the living room and he handed her Mom's acoustic guitar. He had one of his electric guitars plugged in.

"Okay, let's practice the cords we learned last time, together. You play them and when you have found your rhythm, I will improvise and we will see how it turns out."

They played for almost an hour, when her Mom called out from the kitchen. "Soup's on."

They put the guitars away and walked into the kitchen.

"Where's the soup?" Quipped her Dad.

"Very funny. You should be a comedian. I've seen your work, it's funny. Now sit."

Mira and Dad smiled. Dad loved joking with her Mom. They did it all the time, most of the time her Mom bested her Dad. Dinner was a salad, peas and carrots and chicken with mushrooms. There were fresh strawberries for dessert. Her Dad had hulled them for her because she didn't like to have to cut or bite off the stem end. There was only small talk at dinner mostly about the plans for tomorrow. Her Dad had some work to finish up, but promised to meet them at the skating rink and join them for lunch at Jerry's. After dinner her Dad helped her Mom clean up and she told Mira she could watch a video or read until they were finished. Mira chose to read and went to her room. About thirty minutes later, she heard her Mom calling her.

"Coming, Mom."

Mira bookmarked her place and set the book on her desk. Her heart was beating faster as she walked into the den. Her Mom and Dad were sitting on the sofa facing the TV and they pointed to the other matching sofa that was cattycorner to it. Mira sat on the sofa tucking her feet under her for support and looked at her parents. Her Dad had the copy of the National Inquirer on his lap."

"First let me say that your Mom told me that Grandpa Steve called and what he said. I agree with him. So I wouldn't worry about any problems for Nugget. You on the other hand have been doing things we, as concerned and loving parents, feel we should have been told about. After all, we wouldn't what you to end up as pumpkin soup."

Mira smiled, because she could sense now that everything was going to work out. Her Mom rolled her eyes.

"Mira, thinking back on all that happened; I guess I knew you and Jack were up to something. I also think that somehow my Dad is in on this as well. It is just like him. I know that you didn't lie to us, but you omitted things and shaded the story a bit. Didn't you?"

"Yes. Mam."

"It sounds to me like you're going to be grounded for life. No skating, no soccer, no school, no book reading, no eating anything but Lima beans."

"DAD!"

"Okay, now it's time to come clean. We want the whole story from the beginning please and don't leave out any details."

Mira took a deep breath and started her story with Jack's first encounter with the tornado in the park and finished with their most recent adventure. When she was done with her story, there was total silence.

"Well, that's quite a tale. I was sure that was you and Jack at the parade in Norway and now I am sure about the fish smell when you went to Florida. I am proud of you for thinking of going there first. Your Grandfather is an adventurer himself and knows how to get things done. Did you know that he once camped out in the Rocky Mountains in a snow storm by himself to hunt elk?"

"Really?"

"Yes, he has done that and much more. So if he knew and didn't say anything then I think he figured you would be okay. He would never do anything that would put you in jeopardy. Our concern is that you didn't trust us enough to tell us. I'll deal with my Dad later."

"I'm sorry Mom. I guess I felt we could handle it and we didn't want you to tell us no. We planned everything.

"You didn't plan the mine shaft."

"No, not specifically, but we planned ahead for possible problems. We took everything we thought we might need."

There was a minute of silence while her parents looked at each other. They seemed to be able to talk to each other without using words.

"Mira," her Dad said, "you mentioned things like souvenirs. They would certainly prove your stories. Do you have any with you?"

"Yes, sir."

Mira hopped off the sofa and went to her room. She pulled several items out of their hiding places. One she slipped into her pants pocket. She went back into the den and stood in front of her waiting parents.

First she showed them the krona that she got as change in Norway. They each looked at the coins. She said Nugget was from Paradise and they certainly knew him. Then she pulled out the coin that Pope Francis had given her. Her parents were really blown away by that.

"Well that seals it" said her Dad. "And this coin might even get you in to see the Pope when he comes here."

That made Mira smile.

"We believe everything you told us. However, (Ut Oh, here is comes, thought Mira) we don't want you to travel again, (there was a pause and Mira held her breath while her eyes got misty) unless you tell us before you go. We want to know what you are doing and where you are going so that we can back you up if necessary. You must remember that you are eight years old not eighteen, even if you feel older. Do you understand?"

Mira couldn't help herself. She started to cry and ran into her parents arms. This was so much better. She could plan adventures with Jack and not worry about her parents. They would help her and be there if she ever needed anything. This was great.

When they finished hugging, Mira turned to her Mom and said.

"Thank you Mom. You remember when you told me about your summer trip to Rome and how much you enjoyed it. You missed not having a souvenir, right?

"Yes Kiddo, why?"

Mira reach into her pocket and brought out two round discs about the size of a large coffee mug and handed them to her Mom. Her Mom looked at them and her eyes grew wide and then got misty. They were two red drink coasters with the name Café Roma on one side and a picture of the Coliseum on the other. It was the café her Mom had eaten at with her friends when she was a teenager.

After a moment, her Mom wiped her eyes and thanked her. She said that this was the best present she had ever gotten, except for her Dad of course. Her Dad grabbed her and gave her a knuckle head. Then they all laughed.

The rest of the evening passed in a flash and Mira finally went off to bed. After putting on her PJ's she called Jack on the walkie talkie.

"Hi Mira. What's happening? Over."

"We need to talk tomorrow. When can you meet me? Over."

"Anytime, I don't have any plans tomorrow except to take Nugget on a long walk. He needs exercise. Over."

"What about after lunch? I am going skating in the morning. I can walk with you and Nugget if you'll wait for me. Over."

"Sure, I'll see you after lunch. Mira, are we going to talk about another trip? Over."

"Yes. Over and out."

"Great. I'll see you tomorrow. Out."

Epilogue

Skating went better than usual for Mira. Even her skating coach seemed to notice. She remarked about how together Mira was today and so jubilant too. Her Mom just smiled because she knew the real reason that Mira was so happy. She could do the things she wanted to do and had the support of her parents. All she had to do now was find a way to tell Jack.

Lunch was great. Jerry's was busy, but they didn't have to wait. She had two pickles before they brought her the hot dog with French fries and a Black Cherry soda in honor of Grandpa Steve. She had overheard her Mom talking to him last night just after she got in bed. Her Mom was annoyed that he hadn't told her about Mira and Jack visiting him. Then she heard something funny. She said,

"Don't go quoting Herman Hears a Who to me, I don't want to hear a promise is a promise. You could have told us."

There was silence for a short while and then her Mom spoke again.

"Yes, I remember. Okay Dad, you win. I'll talk to you guys on Sunday. We are taking Mira to a movie tomorrow at five o'clock then then out to dinner at King's Fish House in Calabasas. I'll tell her. Love you too. Bye."

When Mira and her parents got home after lunch, Mira ask them if it would be alright to go with Jack to walk Nugget.

"Sure, Kiddo, Just be home by 3:30. We are going to a movie and dinner. We thought you would enjoy seeing the new Disney flick and dinner at King's.

"That would be great Mom. I'll see you later. Thanks."

Mira went over to Jack's and Nugget was waiting at the door carrying his own leash. He also had on a new bandana.

"Hi Jack. I see you gave him a new bandana."

"We have several spares. Mom figured he would tear them or lose them."

"Great, let's walk up to Ventura and visit Mr. Hampshire in the hardware store."

"Oh Boy, tell me you have come up with another adventure. What is it?"

"Jack, how do feel about seeing Mount Everest?"

"Dynamite, I was hoping you would say that."

Just then a stiff breeze began to blow, but just on their side of the street. Jack looked around and told Mira

"I am not doing that. I swear."

"I know Jack. Let me tell you the story of the Wind Maiden named Mariah."

Authors Note

Pope Francis is real. He is the 266th Pope of the Roman Catholic Church and lives in Vatican City which is located in the middle of Rome, Italy. He was born on December 17, 1936 in Buenos Aries, Argentina. His name before he became Pope Francis was Jorge Mario Bergoglio. Before he became a priest he majored in chemistry in college. The Papal Garden is one of his favorite places.

The village of Calingasta is also real and is located at the base of the Andes Mountains in the mid-western part of Argentina.

The book Theodore Boone – Kid Lawyer is the first of a series written by John Grisham and published in 2010. It is a very enjoyable read.

STEPHEN M. MERITT

(Jack and Mira Adventure Series)

Garden of Secrets

Panic in Paradise